Praise for *Learning to Talk*

"Part of her consistent brilliance lies in her attention to ghosts *and* mortgages, the light on the moors *and* 1980s educational policy, adolescent self-discovery *and* irregular accounting. These stories hold worlds as wide as those of her longest novels."

—Sarah Moss, *The New York Times Book Review*

"Those who've delighted for decades in Mantel's fiction revel in her chameleonlike facility with language, her ability effortlessly to evoke wildly diverse characters, settings, and atmospheres. . . . The stories here enable us the more fully to appreciate Mantel's wide-ranging gifts. . . . The overall effect of the collection is of a palimpsest, the powerfully atmospheric evocation of an unhappy mid-twentieth-century childhood in northern England."

—Claire Messud, *Harper's Magazine*

"It's a testament to Mantel's brilliance as an author that even though the moments in these stories are subtle, the book somehow feels epic in its own way. . . . And the result is magnificent. *Learning to Talk* is a lovely book, quiet but intense in its own way, and it proves—once again—that Mantel is one of the finest English-language authors working today."

—NPR

"Mantel brings England alive, writing with detail and intellect."

—*Time*

"Elegant, pitch-perfect sentences . . . Here is a writer who can do anything, anytime, anywhere."

—*Oprah Daily*

"Although best known for her long novels, Mantel has also excelled at short, intensely atmospheric books . . . and here that economy shines, as when she homes in on the telling detail with surgical precision. . . . Mantel was born a poor Northern girl, but she was raised to be a writer who would destroy kingdoms."

—*The Boston Globe*

"Wish Mantel's Wolf Hall award-winning, bestselling trilogy had never come to an end? You'll enjoy her new collection of short stories."

—CNN

"Puts all of the author's skill and style on display."

—*Town & Country*

Also by Hilary Mantel

Every Day Is Mother's Day

Vacant Possession

Eight Months on Ghazzah Street

Fludd

A Place of Greater Safety

A Change of Climate

An Experiment in Love

The Giant, O'Brien

Beyond Black

Wolf Hall

Bring Up the Bodies

The Assassination of Margaret Thatcher

Mantel Pieces

The Mirror & the Light

NONFICTION

Giving Up the Ghost

Ink in the Blood

Learning to Talk

Learning to Talk

Stories

Hilary Mantel

A Holt Paperback
Henry Holt and Company
New York

Holt Paperbacks
Henry Holt and Company
Publishers since 1866
120 Broadway
New York, NY 10271
www.henryholt.com

Distributed in Canada by Raincoast Book Distribution Limited

"King Billy Is a Gentleman" first appeared in *New Writing 1992*, Minerva in association with the British Council, 1992; "Destroyed" first appeared in *Granta* (63), 1998; "Curved Is the Line of Beauty" first appeared in *TLS* (No. 5157), 2002; "Learning to Talk" first appeared in *London Magazine*, 1987; "Third Floor Rising" first appeared in *The Times Magazine*, 2000; "The Clean Slate" first appeared in *Woman & Home*, 2001.

The Library of Congress has cataloged the hardcover edition as follows:

Names: Mantel, Hilary, 1952– author.
Title: Learning to talk : stories / Hilary Mantel.
Description: First U.S. edition. | New York : Henry Holt and Company, 2022.
Identifiers: LCCN 2022001890 (print) | LCCN 2022001891 (ebook) |
ISBN 9781250865366 (hardcover) | ISBN 9781250825148 (ebook)
Subjects: LCSH: Children—Fiction. | LCGFT: Short stories.
Classification: LCC PR6063.A438 L43 2022 (print) | LCC PR6063.A438 (ebook) |
DDC 823/.914—dc23/eng/20220114
LC record available at https://lccn.loc.gov/2022001890
LC ebook record available at https://lccn.loc.gov/2022001891

ISBN: 9781250825131 (trade paperback)

Our books may be purchased in bulk for promotional, educational, or business use. Please contact your local bookseller or the Macmillan Corporate and Premium Sales Department at (800) 221-7945, extension 5442, or by email at MacmillanSpecialMarkets@macmillan.com.

Originally published in hardcover in 2022 by Henry Holt and Company

First Holt Paperbacks Edition 2023

Designed by Meryl Sussman Levavi

Printed in the United States of America

10 9 8 7 6 5 4 3 2 1

Once again with love
to Anne Terese:
and her daughter:
and her daughter.

Contents

Preface

These stories are about childhood and youth. They were pulled together over a period of many years; I choose that strenuous verb because for me, the process of short fiction is full of tension and resistance. The story called "King Billy Is a Gentleman" arrived in seconds with its first line and last line intact, but it took me twelve years to fill in the middle. Stories transmute into other stories; although you don't know this when you write them, they turn out to be rehearsals, interim reports.

All the tales arose out of questions I asked myself about my early years. I cannot say that by sliding my life into a fictional form I was solving puzzles—but at least I was pushing the pieces about. I grew up in the north of England, in a village on the edge of the Peak District in Derbyshire, which is also the setting for my novel *Fludd.* It was an industrial village, with a number of soot-blackened textile mills, its steep streets lined by small cold terraced houses. Like many of the local people, my ancestors had come from Ireland to get work, and though by the time I was alive there was no actual fighting in the streets, the first thing you learned about anyone was their religion. The morals of the Roman Catholic minority were scrutinized from the pulpit, and we all, Protestant and Catholic alike, were policed by gossip.

Despite this, when I was about seven, my mother moved her lover into our house. For the next four years I lived with two fathers. The exact circumstances were so bizarre that, if placed in a story unmodified, they would knock every other element out of it. Hence, in these fictions, visitors turn into fathers, fathers fade away, run away, are left behind; they exist in a kind of fugue state. None of them are my real fathers, and they allow other narrative threads to exist in the space of the same tale. So I would not describe these stories as autobiographical, more as autoscopic. From a distant, elevated perspective, my writing self is looking down at a body reduced to a shell, waiting to be fleshed out by phrases. Its outlines approximate to mine, but there is a penumbra for negotiation.

When I was eleven, a move to a new town left me minus one father and with a new name. The shock of the social transition is described in the title story. It is about social class, snobbery, and the right to be heard, and is true save one or two real-life details. "Third Floor Rising" is about my mother and her late-flowering career, and may fairly be described as memoir. The final story, "The Clean Slate," is about a fictitious mother and daughter, but its geography is real. Relatives of my English grandfather, George Foster, lived in a village which was submerged when a reservoir was created to supply water to the cities of the northwest. Stories of the drowned village, current in my childhood, were my introduction to the swampy territory that lies between history and myth; I have been treading water there ever since.

—HILARY MANTEL,
December 2020

King Billy Is a Gentleman

I cannot get out of my mind, now, the village where I was born, just out of the curl of the city's tentacles. We were too close to the city for a life of our own. There was a regular train service—not one of those where you have to lie in wait and study its habits. But we did not like the Mancunians. "Urban, squat and packed with guile" I suppose was our attitude; we sneered at their back-to-back accents and pitied their physiques. My mother, a staunch Lamarckian, is convinced that Mancunians have disproportionately long arms, as a result of generations of labor at the loom. Until (but this was later) a pink housing estate was slammed up, and they were transplanted in their hundreds, like those trees plucked up for Christmas whose roots are dipped in boiling water—well, until then we did not have much to do with people from town. And yet if you ask me if I was a country boy—no, I wasn't that. Our huddle of stones and slates, scoured by bitter winds and rough gossip tongues, had no claim on rural England, where there is morris dancing and fellowship and olde ale flowing. It was a broken, sterile place, devoid of trees, like a transit camp; and yet with the hopeless permanence that transit camps tend to assume. Snow stood on the hills till April.

We lived at the top of the village, in a house which I considered to be haunted. My father had disappeared. Perhaps it was his presence, long and pallid, which slid behind the door in sweeps of draft and raised the hackles on the terrier's neck. He had been a clerk by profession; crosswords were his hobby, and a little angling: simple card games, and a cigarette-card collection. He left at ten o'clock one blustery March morning, taking his albums and his tweed overcoat and leaving all his underwear; my mother washed it and gave it to a jumble sale. We didn't miss him much, only the little tunes which he used to play on the piano: over and over, "Pineapple Rag."

Then came the lodger. He was from further north, a man with long slow vowels, making a meal out of words we got through quite quickly. The lodger was choleric; his flashpoint was low. He was very, very unpredictable; if you were going to see the shape of the future, you had to watch him carefully, quiet and still, with all your intuitions bristling. When I was older I became interested in ornithology, and I brought into play the expertise I had picked up. Again, that was later; there were no birds in the village, only sparrows and starlings, and a disreputable tribe of pigeons strutting in the narrow streets.

The lodger took an interest in me, getting me outside to kick a football around. But I wasn't a robust child, and though I wanted to please him I hadn't the skill. The ball slipped between my feet, as if it were a small animal. He grew alarmed by my bouts of breathless coughing; mollycoddle, he said, but he said it with fright in his face. Soon he seemed to write me off. I began to feel I was a nuisance. I went to bed early, and lay awake, listening to the banging and shouting downstairs; for the lodger must have quarrels, just as he must have his breakfast. The terrier would begin yelping and grizzling, to keep them company, and then later I would hear my mother run upstairs, sniffling quietly to herself. She would not let the lodger go, I knew, she had set her mind on him. He brought home in his pay packets more money than we had ever had in the house, and whereas when he came at first he would hand over his rent money, now he dropped the whole packet on the table, and my mother would open it with her small pointed fingers, and give him back a few shillings for beer and whatever she thought men needed. He was getting a bonus, she told me, he was getting made up to foreman. He was our chance in life. If I had been a girl she would have confided in me more; but I caught the drift of things. I lay awake still, after the footfalls had stopped, and the dog was quiet, and the shadows crept back into the corners of the room; I dozed, and wished I were unhaunted, and wished for the years to pass in a night so that when I woke up I would be a man. As I began to doze, I dreamed that one day a door would open in the wall; and I would walk through it, and in that land I would be the asthmatic little king. There would be a law against quarreling in the land where I was king. But then, in real life, daylight would come, a Saturday perhaps, and I would have to play in the garden.

The gardens at the back of the houses were long narrow strips, fading by way of ramshackle fences into gray cowpat fields. Beyond the fields were the moors, calm steel-surfaced reservoirs and the neat stripes of light and dark green conifers which mark out the good offices of the Forestry Commission. Little grew in these gardens: scrub grass, tangles of stunted bush, ant-eaten fence poles and lonely strands of wire. I used to go down to the bottom of the garden and pull long rusty nails out of our rotting fence; I used to pull the leaves off the lilac tree, and smell the green blood on my hands, and think about my situation, which was a peculiar one.

Bob and his family had come to live next door to us in some early, singular transplantation from the city. Perhaps this accounted for his attitude to his land. We viewed with distrust the handful of wormy raspberries the garden produced by itself, the miserable lupins running to seed; the straggling rhubarb was never cut and stewed. But Bob had fenced in his garden like the propositions central to a man's soul: as if he had the Holy Grail in his greenhouse, and the Vandals were howling and barracking in the cowpat fields. Bob's garden was military, it was correct; it knew its master. Life grew in rows; things went into the ground out of packets and came up on the dot and stood straight and tall for Bobby's inspection. Unused flowerpots were stacked up like helmets, canes bristled like bayonets. He had possessed and secured every inch of the ground. He was a gaunt man, with a large chin and a vacant blue eye; he never ate white sugar, only brown.

One day over the fence erupted Myra, his wife, about my mother's immoral way of life; twittering in incoherent and long-bottled rage about the example set to her children, to the children of the gardens around. I was eight years old. I fixed her with my very gimlet eye, words of violence bursting into my mouth, contained there swilling and bloody, like loose teeth. I wanted to say that the children of these tracts of ground—her own in particular—were beyond example. My mother, at whom the tirade was directed, got up slowly from the chair where she had been taking the sun; she gave Myra one cursory unregarding glance, and walked silently into the house, leaving her neighbor to hurl herself like a crazed budgerigar at Bob's good fences. Myra was little, she was mere, rat-faced and meager, like a nameless cut in a butcher's window in a demolition area. In my mother's view, her arms hung below her knees.

I think that before this the two households had been quite friendly. Increasingly, then, Bob and his preoccupations (nine bean rows will I have there, a hive for the honeybee) became the butt of our secret sniggers. Bob slunk nightly into the garden, to be away from the stewing-cut his wife. When his mysterious grubbings were done, his drillings and plowings, he stood by the fence and lifted lackluster eyes to the hills, his hands in his pockets; he whistled an air, tuneless and plaintive. From our kitchen he could just be seen, through the clammy evening mists that were the climate of those years. Then my mother would draw the curtains and put the kettle on the gas, and bemoan her life; and she would laugh at Bobby boy, and wonder what damage would be done before he stood there again the next day.

For Bob's fences were not secure. They were elaborate, they were refined, you might say they were highly strung, though this is a strange word to apply to a fence. They were like Stendhal on the shelves of the village library: impressive, but not adapted for any purpose we could discern. The cows would get in; we would watch them nosing softly in the dawn or dusk, lifting Bobby's neat catches with their heads; and trample, they came, slurping and crunching on his succulent produce, satisfying each of their four stomachs, their ruminant eyes mildly joyous with the righteousness of it all.

But Bob had a low opinion of bovine intelligence. For leaving the gates open, he would thrash his son, Philip. From behind our own stone walls we would hear Bobby's demented passions pouring out, his great explosions of grief and despair at the loss of his cucumber frames, wails torn out of his gut. This state of affairs afforded some satisfaction to me. I had some friends; or rather, there were children of my own age.

But because my mother kept me away from school so often—I was sick with this and I was sick with that—I was a strange object to them, and my name, which was Liam, they said was ridiculous. They were wild children, with scabbed knees, and hearts full of fervor, and intolerant mouths and hard eyes; they had rites, they had rules, and they made me an outsider in the tribe. Being ill was almost better; it is something you must do alone.

When I did appear at school, it was seen that I had fallen behind with the lessons. Mrs. Burbage was our teacher, a woman of perhaps fifty, with sparse reddish hair, and fingertips yellow from cigarettes. She told me to stand up and explain the proverb "Never spoil the ship for a ha'pennyworth of tar." In those days that was how children were educated. She carried a bulging tartan bag with her, and each morning deposited it, with a plump thud, on the floor by her desk; then in no time at all the shouting and hitting would begin. It was a tyranny, under which we labored, and while we dreamed of retaliation, a year of our childhood slid by, unnoticed. Some of the children were planning to kill her.

There was nature study; while we sat with our arms folded behind our back, she read to us about the habits of the greenfinch. In spring there was pussy willow, which is thought to be of interest to children everywhere. But it is not spring that I remember: rather those days when the lights were on by eleven o'clock, and wet roofs and the mill chimneys shivered behind a curtain of water. At four o'clock the daylight would almost have vanished, sucked away into the dark sky; our wellingtons squelched in the mud and dead leaves, and breath hung like disaster on the raw air.

The children had been listening in to their parents' gossip. They asked me—the girls especially—searching questions about the sleeping arrangements in our house. I did not see the point of these questions, but I knew better than to answer them. There were fights—scrapping and scratching, nothing serious. "I'll show you how to fight," the lodger said. When I put his advice into practice I left tears and bloody noses. It was the triumph of science over brutality, but it left a sick taste in my mouth, a fear of the future. I would rather run than fight, and when I ran the steep streets turned misty and liquid before my eyes, and the marching fence of my ribs entrapped my heart like a lobster in its pot.

My relations with Bob's children had little to commend them. Quite often, when I was playing outside, Philip and Suzy would come into their own garden and throw stones at me. Looking back, I don't know how there could have been stones in Bobby's garden; not stones just lying about, for use as casual missiles. I suppose if they found any they thought they were doing their father a favor by lobbing them over at me. And as he got stranger, and more persecuted, and ate ever more peculiar foods, no doubt they had to jump at the chance to do him a favor.

Suzy was a hard little madam, with an iron-wide mouth like a postbox; she hung on the gate and taunted. Philip was older than me, perhaps by three years. He had a modified coconut head and a puzzled narrow gray eye, and a sort of sideways motion to his neck, as if constantly in training to avoid the blows he got on account of the cows; perhaps he was concussed. As for the missiles, it didn't give me much trouble to stay out of the small range of his accuracy; but when I evaded him once too often, when I saw I was making him look a fool, I would get myself indoors, because I saw in his face a sort of low destructive rage, as if some other creature might break through, a wilder beast; and it is true that I have seen this look since, on the faces of large intelligent dogs that are kept tied up. And by saying this I do not mean that I thought Philip was an animal, then or now; what I thought was that we all have a buried nature, a secret violence, and I envied the evident power of his skinny sinewy arms, veined and knotted like the arms of a grown man. I envied him, and loathed his subject nature, and I hoped it was not my own. Once I scrabbled for clods of earth and sticks and hurled them back howling like a demon, with all the invective I had at my command from the books I had read: varlet, cuckold, base knave and cur.

As the months passed, Bob grew more vacant in his expression, more dangerous in his rages; his clothes, even, seemed to share his lack of coherence, flapping after him dementedly as if trying to regain the security of the wardrobe. He bought a motor scooter, which broke down every day at the top of the hill, in front of the bus queue. The queue was for the bus to the next village; it was the same people every day. Each morning they were eager for the spectacle. At this stage Philip used to approach the fence and talk to me. Our conversations were wary and elliptical. Did I, he asked, know the names of all the nine planets? Yes, I knew them. He betted, Philip said, I only knew Venus, Mars. I recited them, all nine. The planets have satellites, I told him. Satellites are small things that revolve round big things, I said, held in an orbit by forces beyond themselves; thus Saturn had among others Dione, Titan, Phoebe, and Mars had Deimos, Phobos.

And as I said "Phobos" I felt a catch in my throat, for I knew that the word meant "fear"; and even to speak it was to feel it, and summon up the awkward questions, the lodger, the door in the wall and the shadows of encroaching night.

Then Philip threw stones at me. I went inside and drew pictures sitting at the kitchen table, watching the clock in case the lodger came home.

Now, Philip and I did not attend the same school. Our village had its division, and while the grown-ups were tolerant, or perhaps contemptuous of religion, immersed in football pools and hire-purchase agreements, the children kept up the slanging matches and the chants, the kind of thing you might have heard on Belfast streets, or in Glasgow. Suzy sang out in her tuneless cackle:

"King Billy is a gentleman.
He wears a watch and chain.
The dirty Pope's a beggar
And he begs down our lane."

Irish pigs, Philip said. Bog-hogs. Petrol ran in my veins; my fingers itched for triggers; post offices were fortified behind my eyes. Philip threw stones at me.

My territory was shrinking: not the house, not

the garden, not home and not school. All I owned was the space behind my ribs, and that too was a scarred battleground, the site of sudden debouchments and winter campaigns. I did not tell my mother about the external persecutions. Partly it was because she had enough to bear on her own account; partly because of a sneaking pity invading even my own hard heart, as the misunderstanding about the cows grew keener, and Philip's head shrunk more defensively on to his neck. Bobby took the motor scooter behind the house and kicked it savagely; we no longer knew where our duty lay.

Our neighbor then ceased to keep regular hours. He paced the length of his plot, furrowed, harrowed. He lay in wait: for Philip, for the beasts, for Revelations. He crouched by his fence in a corner, skeletal in his blue overalls. The cows never came, when he watched for them. My mother looked out of the window. Her lips curled. You make your own luck, she said. The neighbors discussed Bobby now. They no longer watched for my father's return; by comparison he lacked interest. Bobby weeded and hoed with one eye over his shoulder. Our circumstances are improving, my mother said: with application, you will go to the grammar school. Her dark shiny hair bounced on her shoulders. We can pay for your uniform, she said;

once we couldn't have managed. I thought, they will ask more probing questions at the grammar school. "Where is my dad?" I asked her. "Where did he go? Did he write you a letter?"

"He may be dead, for all I know," she said. "He may be in purgatory, where they don't have postage stamps."

The year I took my exam for the grammar school Bobby was growing cress in pots. He stood at the front gate, trying to sell it to his neighbors, pressing it upon them as very nutritious. Myra, now, had not even the status of the scrag from the slum carvery; she became like one of the shriveled pods or husks, from dusty glass jars, on which Bob eked out his existence.

The priest came, for the annual Religious Examination; the last time for me. He sat on the headmistress's high chair, his broad feet in their brogues set deliberately on the wooden step. He was old, and his breath labored; there was a faint smell about him, of damp wool, of poultices, of cough linctus and piety. The priest liked trick questions. Draw me a soul, he said. A dim-witted child took the proffered chalk, and marked out on the blackboard a vague kidney shape, or perhaps the sole of a shoe. Ah no, Father said, wheezing gently; ah no, little one, that is the heart.

That year, when I was ten years old, our situation

changed. My mother had been right to bank on the choleric lodger; he was an upwardly mobile man. We departed with him to a neat town where spring came early and cloyed with cherry blossom, and thrushes darted softly on trim lawns. When it rained, these people said, lovely for the gardens; in the village they had taken it as one more bleak affront in the series life offered them. I never doubted that Bob had dwindled away entirely among his mauled lettuce rows, out of grief and bewilderment and iron deficiency, his bones rattled by our departing laughter. About Philip I never thought at all. I wiped him from my mind, as if he had never been. "You must never tell anyone we are not married," my mother said, blithe in her double life. "You must never talk to anyone about your family. It's not their business." You must not taunt over the garden fence, I thought. And the word *phobos* you must never say.

It was only later, when I left home, that I understood the blithe carelessness of the average life—how freely people speak, how freely they live. There are no secrets in their lives, there is no poison at the root. People I met had an innocence, an openness, that was quite foreign to my own nature; or if once it had been native to me, then I had lost it long ago in the evening fogs, in the four o'clock darks, abandoned it in the gardens between the straggling fences and tussocks of grass.

I became a lawyer; one must live, as they say. The whole decade of the sixties went by, and my childhood seemed to belong to some much earlier, grayer world. It was my inner country, visited sometimes in dreams that shadowed my day. The Troubles in Northern Ireland began, and my family fell to quarreling about them, and the newspapers were full of pictures of burned-out shopkeepers, with faces like ours.

I was grown up, qualified, long gone from home, when Philip came back into my life. It was Easter, a sunny morning. The windows were open in the dining room, which overlooked the garden with its striped lawn and rockery; and I was a visitor in my own home, eating breakfast, the toast put into a rack and the marmalade into a dish. How life had altered, altered beyond the power of imagination! Even the lodger had become civilized, in his fashion; he wore a suit, and attended the meetings of the Rotary Club.

My mother, who had grown plump, sat down opposite me and handed me the local newspaper, folded to display a photograph.

"Look," she said, "that Suzy's got married."

I took the newspaper and put down my piece

of toast. I examined this face and figure from my childhood. There she stood, a brassy girl with a bouquet that she held like a cosh. Her big jaw was set in a smile. At her side stood her new husband; a little behind, like tricks of the light, were the bowed, insubstantial forms of her parents. I searched behind them, for a shape I would know: Philip slouching, vaguely menacing, half out of the frame. "Where's her brother?" I said. "Was he there?"

"Philip?" My mother looked up. She sat for a moment with her lips parted, a picture of uncertainty, crumbling a bit of toast under her fingers. "Did nobody tell you? About the accident? I thought I told you. Did I not write to you and let you know?" She pushed her small breakfast aside, and sat frowning at me, as if I had disappointed her. "He died," she said.

"Died? How?"

She dabbed a crumb from the corner of her mouth. "Killed himself." She got up, went to the sideboard, opened a drawer, rummaged under table mats and photographs. "I kept the paper. I thought I'd sent it to you."

I knew I had been pulling away; I knew I had been extracting myself bodily, piece by piece, from my early life. I had missed so much, naturally, and yet I thought I had missed nothing of consequence.

But Philip, dead. I thought of the stones he threw, of the puzzled squint of his eye, of the bruises on his gangling legs below his short trousers.

"It's years now," my mother said.

She sat down again, opposite me at the table, and handed me the paper she had preserved. How quickly newsprint goes yellow; it might have come from a Victorian public library. I turned to read, and read how Philip had blown himself up. All the details from the coroner's court: and the verdict, death by misadventure.

Philip had constructed, in Bobby's garden shed, a sugar and weedkiller bomb. It was a fad of the time, making bombs at home; it had been popularized by events in Belfast. Philip's bomb—the use he had for it was unknown—had blown up in his face. I wondered what he had taken with him in the blast: I pictured the shed splintered, the stacked flowerpots reduced to dust, even the cows in their field lifting bemused heads at the noise. An irrelevant thought slid into my mind, that Ireland had undone him at last; and here I was still alive, one of life's Provisionals, one of the men in the black berets. Philip was the first of my contemporaries to die. I think about him often now. Weedkiller, my brain says back to me: as if it needed replication. I am burning on a slower fuse.

Destroyed

When I was very small, small enough to trip every time on the raised curbstone outside the back door, the dog Victor used to take me for a walk. We would proceed at caution across the yard, my hand plunged deep into the ruff of bristly fur at the back of his neck. He was an elderly dog, and the leather of his collar had worn supple and thin. My fingers curled around it, while sunlight struck stone and slate, dandelions opened in the cracks between paving stones, and old ladies aired themselves in doorways, nodding on kitchen chairs and smoothing their skirts over their knees. Somewhere else, in factories, fields and coal mines, England went dully on.

My mother always said that there is no such thing as a substitute. Everything is intrinsically itself, and unlike any other thing. Everything is just once, and happiness can't be repeated. Children should be named for themselves. They shouldn't be named after other people. I don't agree with that, she said.

Then why did she do it, why did she break her own law? I'm trying to work it out, so meanwhile I have a different story, about some dogs, which perhaps relates to it. If I offer some evidence, will you be the judge?

My mother held her strong views, there's no doubt, because she herself was named after her cousin Clara, who died in a boating accident. If Clara had lived she would have been 107 now. It wasn't anything in her character that made my mother angry about the substitution, because Clara was not known to have had any character. No, what upset her was the way the name was pronounced by the people in our village. Cl-air-air-ra: it came sticky and prolonged out of their mouths, like an extruded rope of glue.

In those days we were all cousins and aunts and great-aunts who lived in rows of houses. We went in and out of each other's doors the whole time. My mother said that in the civilized world people would knock, but though she made this observation over and over, people just gave her a glassy-eyed stare and went on the way they always had. There was a great disjunction between the effect she thought she had on the world, and the effect she actually achieved. I only thought this later. When I was seven I thought she was Sun and Moon. That she was like God, everywhere and always. That she was reading your thoughts, when you were still a poor reader yourself, because you were only up to Far & Wide Readers, Green Book III.

Next door to us in the row lived my aunt Connie. She was really my cousin, but I called her aunt because of her age. All the relationships were mixed up, and you don't need to know about them; only that the dog Victor lived with Connie, and mostly under her kitchen table. He ate a meat pie every day, which Connie bought him specially, walking up the street to buy it. He ate fruit, anything he could get. My mother said dogs should have proper food, in tins.

Victor had died by the time I was seven. I don't remember the day of his death, just a dull sense of cataclysm. Connie was a widow. I thought she always had been. Until I was older I didn't know "widow" meant a husband had once been there. Poor Connie, people said, the loss of her faithful dog is another blow to her.

When I was seven I was given a watch, but for my eighth birthday I had a puppy. When the idea of getting a dog was first proposed, my mother said that she wanted a Pekingese. People gave her the look that they gave her when she suggested that civilized people would knock at the door. The idea of anyone in our village owning a Pekingese was simply preposterous; I knew this already. The inhabitants would have plucked and roasted it.

I said, "It's my birthday, and I would like a dog like Victor."

She said, "Victor was just a mongrel."

"Then I'll have just a mongrel," I said.

I thought, you see, that a mongrel was a breed. Aunt Connie had told me, "Mongrels are very faithful."

I liked the idea of fidelity. Though I had no idea what it implied.

A mongrel, after all, was the cheap option. When the morning of my birthday came I suppose I felt excitement, I don't know. A young boy fetched the puppy from Godber's farm. It stood blinking and shivering on the rug before the fire. Its tiny legs were like chicken bones. I am a winter-born person and there was frost on the roads that day. The puppy was white, like Victor, and had a curly tail like Victor, and a brown saddle on his back which made him look useful and domestic. I put my hand into the fur at the back of his neck and I judged that one day it would be strong enough to hang on to.

The boy from Godber's farm was in the kitchen, talking to my stepfather, who I was told to call Dad these days. I heard the boy say it was a right shame, but I didn't listen to find out what the shame was. The boy went out, my stepfather with him. They were chatting as if they were familiar.

I didn't understand in those days how people knew each other. They'd say, you know *her*, *her* who married *him*. Constant was her name before she married him, or, her name was Reilly. There was a time when I didn't understand how names got changed, or how anything happened, really. When somebody went out of the door I always wondered who or what they'd come back as, and whether they'd come back at all. I don't mean to make me sound simple, my infant self. I could pick out reasons for everything I did. I thought it was other people who were the sport of fortune, and the children of whim. I was the sole heir to the logic in my head: sole heir and beneficiary.

When my stepfather had gone out, I found myself alone in our front room, before the slumbering and low-burning fire; and so I started talking to the puppy Victor. I had read manuals of dog training in preparation for his arrival. They said that dogs liked a low, calm, soothing tone, but they didn't suggest what to say in it. He didn't look as if he had many interests yet, so I told him about the things that interested me. I squatted on the floor next to him, so my great size wouldn't intimidate him. I looked into his face. Know my face, I prayed. After a certain amount of boredom from me, Victor fell to the floor as if his legs had been snapped, and slept like the dead. I sat down beside him to watch him. I had a book open on my knees but I didn't read it. I watched him, and I had never been so still. I knew that fidgeting was a vice, and I had tried to combat it, but I did not know stillness like that was in me, or calm like in the half hour I first watched Victor.

When my stepfather came back, he had a worried frown on his face, and something under his overcoat. A foxy muzzle poked out, noisily snuffling the air. "This is Mike," my stepfather said. "He was going to be destroyed." He put the new puppy on the ground. It was a bouncing skewbald made of rubber. It ran to the fire. It ran to Victor and sniffed him. It raced in a circle and bit chunks out of the air. Its tongue panted. It jumped on Victor and began to pulverize him.

Mike—let it be understood—was not an extra present for me. Victor was my dog and my responsibility. Mike was the *other* dog: he was everyone's, and no one's, responsibility. Victor, as it proved, was of sedate, genteel character. When he was first put on his lead, he walked daintily, at heel, as if he had been trained in a former life.

But when the lead was first clipped on to Mike's collar, he panicked. He ran to the end of it and yelped and spun into the air, and hurtled out into space, and turned head over heels. Then he flopped down on his side, and thrashed around as if he were in danger of a heart attack. I fumbled at his collar, desperate to set him free; his eye rolled, the fur of his throat was damp.

Try him again, when he's a bit older, my mother suggested.

Everybody said that it was nice that Victor had got his brother with him, that they would be faithful to each other, etc. I didn't think so, but what I didn't think I kept to myself.

The puppies had a pretty good life, except at night when the ghosts that lived in our house came out of the stone-floored pantry, and down from the big cupboard to the left of the chimney breast. Depend upon it, they were not dripping or ladies or genteel; they were nothing like the ghost of drowned Clara, her sodden blouse frilled to the neck. These were ghosts with filed teeth. You couldn't see them, but you could sense their presence when you saw the dogs' bristling necks, and saw the shudders run down their backbones. The ruff on Victor's neck was growing long now. Despite everything my mother had vowed, the dogs did not get food out of tins. They got scraps of anything that was going. Substitutions were constantly made, in our house. Though it was said that no one thing was like any other.

"Try the dog on his lead again," my mother said. If a person said, "the dog," you knew Mike was the dog meant. Victor sat in the corner. He did not impose his presence. His brown eyes blinked.

I tried the dog on his lead again. He bolted across the room, taking me with him. I borrowed a book from the public library, *101 Hints on Dog Care*. Mike took it in the night and chewed it up, all but the last four hints. Mike would pull you in a hedge, he would pull you in a canal, he would pull you in a boating lake so you drowned like cousin Clara, when her careless beau tipped her out of the rowing boat. When I was nine I used to think quite a lot about Clara, her straw hat skimming among the lily pads.

It was when my brother P.G. Pig was born that my mother broke her own rule. I heard the cousins and aunts talking in lowered voices about the choice of name. They didn't take my views into account—no doubt they thought I'd recommend, Oh, call him Victor. Robert was mooted but my mother said Bob she could not abide. All those names were at first to be ruled out, that people naturally make into something else. But this left too few to draw on. At last my mother made up her mind on Peter, both syllables to be rigidly enforced. How did she think she would enforce them when he was a schoolboy, when he went to the football field, when he grew to be a weaver or a soldier in a khaki blouson? I asked myself these things. And, mentally, I shrugged. I saw myself in my mind. "Just asking!" I said. My fingers were spread and my eyes were round.

But there was something else about the baby's name, something that was going to be hidden. By listening at doors, by pasting myself against the wall and listening at doors, I found it was this; that the baby was to be given a second name, and it was to be George, which was the name of my aunt Connie's dead husband. Oh, had Connie a husband, I said to myself. I still thought that widow, like mongrel, was a category of its own.

Peter George, I said to myself, PG, Peegee, P.G. Pig. He would have a name, and it would not be Peter, nor would it be Pete. But why so hushed? Why the averted shoulders and the voices dropped? *Because Connie was not to be told.* It was going to be too much for her altogether, it would send her into a fit of the hysterics if she found out. It was my own mother's personal tribute to the long-destroyed George, who to my knowledge she had not mentioned before: a tribute which, to pay, she was prepared to throw over one of her most characteristic notions. So strong, she said, were her feelings on the matter.

But wait. Wait a minute. Let logic peep in at the window here. This was Connie, was it not? Aunt Connie who lived next door? It was Connie, who in three weeks' time would attend the christening? As Catholics we christen early, being very aware of the devil. I pictured the awful word "George" weighting the priest's tongue, making him clutch his upper chest, reducing him to groans until it rolled out, crashing on the stone floor and processing down the aisle; and Connie's arm flung up, the word "Aa . . . gh!" flashing from her gaping mouth as she was mown down. What an awful death, I said to myself. Smirking, I said, what a destruction.

In the event, Connie found out about the naming in good time. My mother said—and thunder was on her brow—"They told her in the butcher's. And she'd only gone in, bless her, for her little bit of a slice of—"

I left her presence. In the kitchen, Victor was sitting in the corner, curling up an edge of liver-colored lip. I wondered if something had provoked him. A ghost come out early? Perhaps, I thought, it's George.

Connie was next door as usual, going about her tasks in her own kitchen. You could hear her through the thin wall; the metal colander knocking against the enamel sink, the squeak of chair legs across the linoleum. In the days following she showed no sign of hysterical grief, or even nostalgia. My mother watched her closely. "They never should have told her," my mother said. "A shock such as that could do lasting harm." For some reason, she looked disappointed.

I didn't know what it was about, and I don't now, and I doubt if I want to: it was just some tactic one person was trying on another person and it was the reason I didn't like to play cat's cradle, patience, cutting out with scissors or any indoor games at all. Winter or not, I played outside with Victor and Mike.

It was spring when P.G. Pig was born. I went out into the field at the back, to get away from the screaming and puking and baby talk. Victor sat quivering at my heel. Mike raced in insane circles among the daisies. I pushed back my nonexistent cowboy hat. I scratched my head like an old-timer and said, "Loco."

My brother was still a toddler when Victor's character took a turn for the worse. Always timid, he now became morose, and took to snapping. One day when I came to put on his lead he sprang into the air and nipped me on the cheek. Believing myself an incipient beauty and afraid of facial scarring, I washed the bite then rubbed raw Dettol on it. What resulted was worse than the bite and I rehearsed to the air the sentence "Hurts like hell." I tried not to tell my mother but she smelled the Dettol.

Later, he chased P.G. Pig, trying to get him on the calf. PG marched to the German goosestep. So, he escaped by inches, or even less. I plucked a raveled thread of his toweling suit from between Victor's teeth.

Victor didn't attack grown people. He backed off from them. "It's just the children he goes for," my mother said. "I find it very perplexing."

So did I. I wondered why he included me with the children. If he could see into my heart, I thought, he would know I don't qualify.

By this time we had a new baby in the house. Victor was not to be trusted and my mother said a sorting-out was overdue. He went away under my stepfather's overcoat, wrapped tight, struggling. We said goodbye to him. He was pinioned while we patted his head. He growled at us, and the growl turned to a snarl, and he was hurried out of the front door, and away down the street.

My mother said that she and my father had found a new home for him, with an elderly couple without children. How sad! I pictured them, their homely grieving faces softening at the sight of the white dog with his useful brown saddle. He would be a substitute child for them. Would they dip their old fingers into the ruff at his neck, and hold on tight?

It was strange, what I chose to believe in those days. P.G. Pig knew better. Sitting in the corner, he took a sideways swipe at his tower of blue bricks. "Destroyed," he said.

About a year after that, we moved to a new town. My surname was changed officially. Pig and the younger baby had the new name already, there was no need for them to change. My mother said that generally, the gossip and malice had got out of hand, and there were always those who were ready to do you a bad turn if they could contrive it. Connie and the other aunts and cousins came to visit. But not too often. My mother said, we don't want *that* circus starting up again.

So the years began in which I pretended to be someone else's daughter. The word "daughter" is long, pale, mournful; its hand is to its cheek. The word "rueful" goes with "daughter." Sometimes I thought of Victor and I was rueful. I sat in my room with compass and square-ruled book and bisected angles, while outside the children shrieked, frolicking with Mike. In truth I blamed Mike for alienating Victor's affections, but there is a limit to how much you can blame a dog.

With the move to the new house, a change had overtaken Mike, similar in magnitude though not in style to the one that had overtaken his brother x years before. I call it x years because I was beginning to lose track of that part of my life, and in the case of numbers it is allowable to make a substitution. I remembered the facts of things pretty well, but I had forgotten certain feelings, like how I felt on the day Victor arrived from Godber's farm, and how I felt on the day he was taken away to his new home. I remembered his straitjacketed snarling, which hardly diminished as he was carried out of the door. If he could have bitten me that day, he would have drawn blood.

The trouble with Mike was this: we had become middle class, but our dog had not. We had long ago ceased trying to take him for walks on a lead. Now he exercised himself, running away at all hours of the day and night. He could leap gates and make holes through hedges. He was seen in the vicinity of butchers' shops. Sometimes he went to the high street and stole parcels and packets from baskets on wheels. He ate a white loaf, secretly, in the shadow of the privet. I saw that he looked dedicated and innocent as he chewed it, slice after slice, holding the dough carefully in paws that he turned inward, as if praying.

When my mother saw the neighbors leaning over the larch-lap, imparting gardening tips, she thought they were talking about Mike. Her face would become pinched. She believed he was letting the family down, betraying mongrel origins. I knew the meaning of the word now. I did not get involved in any controversy about Mike. I crouched in my room and traced the continent of South America. I stuck into my geography book a picture of Brasília, the white shining city in the jungle. I placed my hands together and prayed, take me there. I did not believe in God so I prayed provisionally, to genies and ghosts, to dripping Clara and old dead George.

Mike was less than five years old when he began to show his age. He had lived hard, after all. One year, he could catch and snap in his jaws the windfalls our apple tree shook down. Those he did not catch as they fell, the babies would bowl for him, and he would hurtle after, tearing skid marks in the turf as he cornered; then with a backward jerk of his neck he would toss the fruit up into the blue air, to give himself a challenge.

But a year later, he was on the blink. He couldn't catch the windfalls if they rained down on his head, and when old tennis balls were thrown for him he would trot vaguely, dutifully, away from the hue and cry, and then turn and plod back, his jaws empty. I said to my mother, I think Mike's eyes are failing. She said, I hadn't noticed.

The defect didn't seem to make him downhearted. He continued to lead his independent life; smelling his way, I supposed, through gaps in wire netting and through the open doors of vendors of fine foods and High Class Family Butchers. I thought, he could do with a guide person really. Perhaps I could train up P.G. Pig? I tried the experiment we hadn't tried in years, clipping lead to collar. The dog lay down at my feet and whimpered. I noticed that the foxy patches of his coat had bleached out, as if he'd been in the sun and the rain too long. I unfastened the lead and wrapped it around my hand. Then I threw it at the back of the hall cupboard. I stood in the hall and practiced swearing under my breath. I didn't know why.

On New Year's Day, a fortnight before my twelfth birthday, Mike went out in the morning and didn't come back. My stepfather said, "Mike's not come in for his tea." I said, "Mike's bloody blind."

They all pretended not to have heard me. There was an edict against quarreling anywhere near Christmas, and it was still near enough; we were lodged in the strange-menu days leading to the Feast of the Epiphany, when babies daub jelly in their hair and *The Prisoner of Zenda* is on TV and no one notices what time it is. That's why we were less alarmed than we would usually have been, yawning off to bed.

But I woke up very early, and stood shivering by the window, the curtain wrapped around me, looking out over land that was imagined because there was no light: leafless, wet, warm for the time of year. If Mike were home I would feel it, I thought. He would whine and buffet the back door, and someone would hear if not me. But I didn't know. I couldn't trust that. I ran my hand through my hair and made it stand up in tufts. I crept back to bed.

I had no dreams. When I woke up it was nine o'clock. I was astonished at the leniency. My mother needs little sleep, and thinks it a moral failing in others, so usually she would have been bawling in my ear by eight, inventing tasks for me; the Christmas truce did not apply in the earlier hours of the morning. I went downstairs in my spotted pajamas, the legs rolled up above the knee, in a *jeu d'esprit.*

"Oh, for God's sake," my mother said. "And what have you done with your hair?"

I said, "Where's my dad?"

She said, "He's gone to the police station, about Mike."

"No," I said. I shook my head. I rolled down my pajama trousers to the ankle. Fuckit, I wanted to say, I mean my dad, I don't mean the substitute. *Answer the question I put to you.*

The next day I went out calling, through the small woods that belted open fields, and along the banks of the canal. It rained part of the day, a benign and half-hearted precipitation. Everything seemed unseasonable, forward: the rotting wood of fences shimmered green. I took my redoubtable brother with me, and I kept my eye on the yellow bobble of his bobble hat. The minute he went out of sight, in undergrowth or copse, I called him, Peegee Pig! I felt him before I saw him, loping to my side.

I had penny chews in my pocket and I fed them to him to keep him going. "Mike, Mike!" we called. It was Sunday, the end of an extended holiday which had added to the dislocation of Advent. We met no one on our quest. Peegee's nose began to run. After a time, when the dog didn't answer, he began to cry. He'd thought we were going to meet Mike, you see. At some place prearranged.

I just tugged Peegee along. It was all I could do. The word "interloper" was rolling around my mind, and I thought what a beautiful word it was, and how well it described the dog Mike who loped and flapped his pink tongue in the open air, while Victor squatted in the house, incubating fear; and I could not help him, because I shared it and it was the only thing I could give him to eat.

On the banks of the canal at last we met a man, not old, his jacket flapping and insufficient even for the mildness of the day; his hair cropped, his torn pocket drooping from his checked shirt, and his gym shoes caked in mud. Who was Mike? he wanted to know.

I told him my mother's theory, that Mike had been mowed down by a Drunken Driver. Peegee sawed his hand back and forth under his snuffling nose. The man promised he would call out for Mike, and take him if recovered to the police or the RSPCA. Beware of the police pounds, he said, for the dogs there are destroyed in twelve days.

I said that within twelve days we would be sure

to hear from them. I said, my step my step my *father* has been to the police: I managed the word in the end. I swear by Almighty God, the man said, that I will be calling for young Michael day and night. I felt alarmed for him. I felt sorry for his torn pocket, as if I should have been carrying needle and thread.

I walked away, and I had not gone a hundred yards before I felt there were misunderstandings that needed to be corrected. Mike is only my stepdog. Supposing I had misinformed this stranger? But if I went back to put the facts to him again, perhaps he would only forget them. He looked like a man who had forgotten almost everything. I had gone another hundred yards before it came to me that this was the very kind of stranger to whom you were warned not to speak.

I looked down at Peegee in secondhand alarm. I should have protected him. Peegee was learning to whistle that week, and now he was whistling and crying at the same time. He was whistling the tune from Laurel and Hardy, which I can't stand. I knew full well—"full well" is one of my mother's expressions—that Mike was dead in a ditch, where he had limped or crawled away from the vehicle that had smashed him up before he saw it. All day I'd been searching, in defiance of this fact.

Oh, I'm tired, Peegee wailed. Carry me. Carry me. I looked down and knew I could not, and he knew it too, for he was such a big boy already that it could almost have been the other way around. I offered him a penny chew, and he smacked my hand away.

We came to a wall, and I hoisted him on to it. He could have hoisted me. We sat there, while the air darkened. It was four o'clock, and we had been walking and calling since early morning. I thought, I could drown Peegee Pig, and blame it on the man with the torn pocket. I could haul him across the towpath by the hood of his coat, and push him under the bright green weed; and keep pushing, a hand on his face, till the weight of his clothes pulled him under; and I saw myself, careless beau, other life, lily pad and floating hat. As far as I knew, no one had been hanged for Clara. "What's for my tea?" Peegee said. Some words came to me, from the Shakespeare we were doing: When the exigent should come—which now is come indeed . . . The damp was making me ache, as if I were my own grandmother. I thought, nobody listens, nobody sees, nobody does any bloody fuckit thing. You go blind and savage and they carry on making Christmas trifles and frying eggs. Fuckit, I said to Peegee, experimentally. Fuckit, he repeated after me. Mike, Mike, we called, as we trod the towpath, and early night closed in on us. Peegee Pig slipped his hand into mine. We walked into the dark together, and our fused hands were cold. I said, to myself, I cannot kill him, he is fidelity itself; though it did occur to me that if he drowned, someone would be named after him. "Come on, Peegee," I said to him. "But cut out the whistling." I stood behind him, put my cold hands into the hood of his duffel coat, and began to steer him home.

There was a lot of blame flying in the air, about where had we been, up by the canal where vagrants live and anybody. My mother had already washed Mike's dishes out, and put them to drain. As she was not much of a housewife, we knew by this sign that he was not coming back, not through our door anyway. I cried a bit then, not out of the exhaustion of the day, but sudden scorching tears that leaped out of my eyes and scoured the pattern off the wallpaper. I saw Peegee gaping at me, open-mouthed, so I was sorry I'd bothered crying at all. I just wiped my fist across my face, and got on with the next thing.

Curved Is the Line of Beauty

wetness underfoot, its scaly patches of late snow, and the tossing inland squall that was its typical climate. Even in mild weather its air was wandering, miasmic, like memories that no one owns. When raw drizzle and fog invaded the streets of the peripheral settlements, it was easy to feel that if you stepped out of your family house, your street, your village, you were making a risky move; one mistake, and you would be lost.

The other way of being lost, when I was a child, was by being damned. Damned to hell that is, for all eternity. This could happen very easily if you were a Catholic child in the 1950s. If the speeding driver caught you at the wrong moment—let us say, at the midpoint between monthly confessions—then your dried-up soul could snap from your body like a dead twig. Our school was situated handily, so as to increase the risk, between two bends in the road. Last-moment repentance is possible, and stress was placed on it. You might be saved if, in your final welter of mashed bones and gore, you remembered the correct formula. So it was really all a matter of timing. I didn't think it might be a matter of mercy. Mercy was a theory that I had not seen in operation. I had only seen how those who wielded power extracted maximum advantage from every situation. The politics of the playground and classroom are as instructive as those of the parade ground and the Senate. I understood that, as Thucydides would later tell me, "the strong exact what they can, and the weak yield what they must."

Accordingly, if the strong said, "We are going to Birmingham," to Birmingham you must go. We were going to make a visit, my mother said. To whom, I asked; because we had never done this before. To a family we had not met, she said, a family we did not yet know. In the days after the announcement I said the word "family" many times to myself, its crumbly soft sound like a rusk in milk, and I carried its scent with me, the human warmth of checkered blankets and the yeast smell of babies' heads.

In the week before the visit, I went over in my mind the circumstances that surrounded it. I challenged myself with a few contradictions and puzzles which these circumstances threw up. I analyzed who *we* might be, we who were going to make the visit: because that was not a constant or a simple matter.

The night before the visit I was sent to bed at eight—even though it was the holidays and Saturday next day. I opened the sash window and leaned out into the dusk, waiting till a lonely string of street-lights blossomed, far over the fields, under the upland shadow. There was a sweet grassy fragrance, a haze in the twilight; *Dr. Kildare*'s Friday-night theme tune floated out from a hundred TV sets, from a hundred open windows, up the hill, across the reservoir, over the moors; and as I fell asleep I saw the medics in their frozen poses, fixed, solemn and glazed, like heroes on the curve of an antique jar.

I once read of a jar on which this verse was engraved:

> Straight is the line of duty;
> Curved is the line of beauty.
> Follow the straight line; thou shalt see
> The curved line ever follow thee.

At five o'clock, a shout roused me from my dreams. I went downstairs in my blue spotted pajamas to wash in hot water from the kettle, and I saw the outline of my face, puffy, in the light like gray linen tacked to the summer window. I had never been so far from home; even my mother had never, she said, been so far. I was excited and excitement made me sneeze. My mother stood in the kitchen in the first uncertain shaft of sun, making sandwiches with cold bacon and wrapping them silently, sacramentally, in greaseproof paper.

We were going in Jack's car, which stood the whole

night, these last few months, at the curb outside our house. It was a small gray car, like a jelly mold, out of which a giant might turn a foul jelly of profanity and grease. The car's character was idle, vicious and sneaky. If it had been a pony you would have shot it. Its engine spat and steamed, its underparts rattled; it wanted brake shoes and new exhausts. It jibbed at hills and sputtered to a halt on bends. It ate oil, and when it wanted a new tire there were rows about having no money, and there was slamming the door so hard that the glass of the kitchen cupboard rattled in its grooves.

The car brought out the worst in everybody who saw it. It was one of the first cars on the street, and the neighbors, in their mistaken way, envied it. Already sneerers and ill-wishers of ours, they were driven to further spite when they saw us trooping out to the curb carrying all the rugs and kettles and camping stoves and raincoats and wellington boots that we took with us for a day at the seaside or the zoo.

There were five of *us*, now. Me and my mother; two biting, snarling, pinching little boys; Jack. My father did not go on our trips. Though he still slept in the house—the room down the corridor, the one with the ghost—he kept to his own timetables and routines, his Friday jazz club, and his solitary sessions of syncopation, picking at the piano, late weekend afternoons, with a remote gaze. This had not always been his way of life. He had once taken me to the library. He had taken me out with my fishing net. He had taught me card games and how to read a racecard; it might not have been a suitable accomplishment for an eight-year-old, but any skill at all was a grace in our dumb old world.

But those days were now lost to me. Jack had come to stay with us. At first he was just a visitor and then without transition he seemed to be always there. He never carried in a bag, or unpacked clothes; he just came complete as he was. After his day's work he would drive up in the evil car, and when he came up the steps and through the front door, my father would melt away to his shadowy evening pursuits. Jack had sunburned skin and muscles beneath his shirt. He was your definition of a man, if a man was what caused alarm and shattered the peace.

To amuse me, while my mother combed the tangles out of my hair, he told me the story of David and Goliath. It was not a success. He tried his hardest—as I tried also—to batten down my shrieks. As he spoke his voice slid in and out of the London intonations with which he had been born; his brown eyes flickered, caramel and small, the whites jaundiced. He made the voice of Goliath, but—to my mind—he was lacking in the David department.

After a long half hour, the combing was over. My vast weight of hair studded to my skull with steel clips, I pitched exhausted from the kitchen chair. Jack stood up, equally exhausted, I suppose; he would not have known how often this needed to happen. He liked children, or imagined he did. But (owing to recent events and my cast of mind) I was not exactly a child, and he himself was a very young man, too inexperienced to navigate through the situation in which he had placed himself, and he was always on the edge, under pressure, chippy and excitable and quick to take offense. I was afraid of his flaring temper and his irrationality: he argued with brute objects, kicked out at iron and wood, cursed the fire when it wouldn't light. I flinched at the sound of his voice, but I tried to keep the flinch inward.

When I look back now I find in myself—in so far as I can name what I find—a faint stir of fellow feeling that is on the way to pity.

It was Jack's quickness of temper, and his passion for the underdog, that was the cause of our trip to Birmingham. We were going to see a friend of his, who was from Africa. You will remember that we have barely reached the year 1962, and I had never seen anyone from Africa, except in photographs, but the prospect in itself was less amazing to me than the knowledge that Jack had a friend. I thought friends were for children. My mother seemed to think that you grew out of them. Adults did not have friends. They had relatives. Only relatives came to your house. Neighbors might come, of course. But not to our house. My mother was now the subject of scandal and did not go out. We were all the subject of scandal, but some of us had to. I had to go to school, for instance. It was the law.

It was six in the morning when we bundled into the car, the two little boys dropped sleep-stunned beside me on to the red leather of the backseat. In those days it took a very long time to get anywhere. There were no motorways to speak of. Fingerposts were still employed, and we did not seem to have the use of a map. Because my mother did not know left from right, she would cry "That way, that way!" whenever she saw a sign and happened to read it. The car would swerve off in any old direction and Jack would start cursing and she would shout back. Our journeys usually found us bogged in the sand at Southport, or broken down by the drystone wall of some Derbyshire beauty spot, the lid of the vile spitting engine propped open, my mother giving advice from the wound-down window: fearful advice, which went on till Jack danced with rage on the roadway or on the uncertain sand, his voice piping in imitation of a female shriek; and she, heaving up the last rags of self-control, heaving them into her arms like some dying diva's bouquet, would drop her voice an octave and claim, "I don't talk like that."

But on this particular day, when we were going to Birmingham, we didn't get lost at all. It seemed a miracle. At the blossoming hour of ten o'clock, the weather still fine, we ate our sandwiches, and I remember that first sustaining bite of salted fat, sealing itself in a plug to the hard palate: the sip of Nescafé to wash it down, poured steaming from the flask. In some town we stopped for petrol. That too passed without incident.

I rehearsed, in my mind, the reason behind the visit. The man from Africa, the friend, was not now but had once been a workmate of Jack. And they had spoken. And his name was Jacob. My mother had told me, don't say "Jacob is black," say "Jacob is colored."

What, colored? I said. What, striped? Like the towel which, at that very moment, was hanging to dry before the fire? I stared at it; the stripes had run together to a patchy violet-gray. I felt it; the fibers were stiff as dried grass. Black, my mother said, is not the term polite people use. And stop mauling that towel!

So now, the friend, Jacob. He had been, at one time, living in Manchester, working with Jack. He had married a white girl. They had gone to get lodgings. At every door they had been turned away. No room at the inn. Though Eva was expecting. Especially because she was expecting. Even the stable door was bolted, it was barred against them. NO COLOREDS, the signs said.

Oh, merrie England! At least people could spell in those days. They didn't write NO COLORED'S or "NO" COLOREDS. That's about all you can say for it.

So: Jacob unfolded to Jack this predicament of his: no house, the insulting notices, the pregnant Eva. Jack, quickly taking fire, wrote a letter to a tabloid newspaper. The newspaper, quick to spot a cause, took fire also. There was naming and shaming; there was a campaign. Letters were written and questions were asked. The next thing you knew, Jacob had moved to Birmingham, to a new job. There was a house now, and a baby, indeed two. Better days were here. But Jacob would never forget how Jack had taken up the cudgels. That, my mother said, was the phrase he had used.

David and Goliath, I thought. My scalp prickled, and I felt steel pins cold against it. Last night had been too busy for the combing. My hair fell smoothly down my back, but hidden above the nape of my neck there was a secret pad of fuzziness which, if slept on for a second night, would require a howling hour to unknot.

The house of Jacob was built of brick in a quiet color of brown, with a white-painted gate and a tree in a tub outside. One huge window stared out at a grass verge, with a sapling; and the road curved away, lined with similar houses, each in their own square of garden. We stepped out of the heat of the car and stood jelly-legged on the verge. Behind the plate glass was a stir of movement, and Jacob opened the front door to us, his face breaking into a smile. He was a tall slender man, and I liked the contrast of his white shirt with the soft sheen of his skin. I tried hard not to say, even to think, the term that is not the one polite people use. Jacob, I said to myself, is quite a dark lavender, verging on purple on an overcast day.

Eva came out from behind him. She had a compensatory pallor, and when she reached out, vaguely patting at my little brothers, she did it with fingers like rolled dough. Well, well, the adults said. And, this is all very nice. Lovely, Eva. And fitted carpets. Yes, said Eva. And would you like to go and spend a penny? I didn't know this phrase. Wash your hands, my mother said. Eva said, run upstairs, poppet.

At the top of the stairs there was a bathroom, not an arrangement I had reason to take for granted. Eva ushered me into it, smiling, and clicked the door behind her. Standing at the basin and watching myself in the mirror, I washed my hands carefully with Camay soap. Maybe I was dehydrated from the journey, for I didn't seem to need to do anything else. I hummed to myself, "You'll look a little lovelier . . . each day . . . with fabulous pink *Camay*." I didn't look around much. Already I could hear them on the stairs, shouting that it was their turn. I dried carefully between my fingers with the towel behind the door. There was a bolt on this door and I thought for a moment of bolting myself in. But a familiar pounding began, a headbutting, a thudding and a giggling, and I opened the door so that my brothers fell in at it and I went downstairs to do the rest of the day.

Everything had been fine, till the last hour of the journey. "Not long to go," my mother had said, and suddenly swiveled in her seat. She watched us, silent, her neck craning. Then she said, "When we are visiting Jacob, don't say 'Jack.' It's not suitable. I want you to say," and here she began to struggle with words, "'Daddy . . . Daddy Jack.'"

Her head, once more, faced front. Studying the line of her cheek, I thought she looked sick. It had been a most unconvincing performance. I was almost embarrassed for her. "Is this just for today?" I asked. My voice came out cold. She didn't answer.

WHEN I GOT back into the downstairs room they were parading Eva's children, a toddler and a baby, and remarking that it was funny how it came out, so you had one butter-colored and one bluish, and Jacob was saying, too, that it was funny how it came out and you couldn't ever tell, really, it was probably beyond the scope of science as we know it today. The sound of a pan rocking on the gas jet came from the kitchen, and there was a burst of wet steam, and some clanking; Eva said, carrots, can't take your eye off them. Wiping her hands on her apron, she made for the door and melted into the steam. My eyes followed her. Jacob smiled and said, so how is the man who took up the cudgels?

WE CHILDREN ATE in the kitchen—my family, that is, because the two babies sat in their own high chairs by Eva and sucked gloop from a spoon. There was a little red table with a hinged flap, and Eva propped the back door open so that the sunlight from the garden came in. We had vast pale slices of roast pork, and gravy that was beige and so thick it kept the shape of the knife. Probably if I am honest about what I remember, I think it is the fudge texture of this gravy that stays in my mind, better even than the afternoon's choking panic, the tears and prayers that were now only an hour or so away.

After our dinner Tabby came. She was not a cat but a girl, and the niece of Jacob. Inquiries were made of me: did I like to draw? Tabby had brought a large bag with her, and from it she withdrew sheets of rough colored paper and a whole set of colored pencils, double-ended. She gave me a quick, modest smile, and a flicker of her eyes. We settled down in a corner, and began to make each other's portrait.

Out in the garden the little boys grubbed up worms, shrieked, rolled the lawn with each other and laid about with their fists. I thought that the two babies, now snorting in milky sleep, would be doing the same thing before long. When one of the boys fetched the other a harder clout than usual, the victim would howl, "Jack! Jack!"

My mother stood looking over the garden. "That's a lovely shrub, Eva," she said. I could see her through the angle made by the open door of the kitchen, her high-heeled sandals planted squarely on the lino. She was smaller than I had thought, when I saw her beside the floury bulk of Eva, and her eyes were resting on something further than the shrub: on the day when she would leave the moorland village behind her, and have a shrub of her own. I bent my head over the paper and attempted the blurred line of Tabby's cheek, the angle of neck to chin. The curve of flesh, its soft bloom, eluded me; I lolled my pencil point softly against the paper, feeling I wanted to roll it in cream, or in something vegetable-soft but tensile, like the fallen petal of a rose. I had already noticed, with interest, that Tabby's crayons were sharpened down in a similar pattern to the ones I had at home. She had little use for gravy color and still less for bl°°k. Almost as unpopular was the double-ended crayon in morbid mauve/dark pink. Most popular with her was gold/green: as with me. On those days when I was tired of crayoning, and started to play that the crayons were soldiers, I had to imagine that gold/green was a drummer boy, so short was he.

On the rough paper, my pencil snagged; at once, my reverie was interrupted. I took in a breath. I bit my lip. I felt my heart begin to beat: an obscure insult, trailing like the smell of old vegetable water, seemed to hang in the air. This paper is for kids, I thought; it's for babies who don't know how to draw. My fingers gripped the crayon. I held it like a dagger. My hand clenched around it. At my toppest speed, I began to execute cartoon men, with straight jointless limbs, and brown *O*'s for heads, with wide grinning mouths, jug ears; petty Goliaths with slatted mouths, with five finger bones splaying from their wrists.

Tabby looked up. Shh, shh . . . she said; as if soothing me.

I drew children rolling in the grass, children made of two circles with a third "O" for their bawling mouths.

Jacob came in, laughing, talking to Jack over his shoulder, ". . . so I tell him, if you want a trained draftsman for £6 a week, man, you can whistle for him!"

I thought, I won't call Jack anything, I won't give him a name. I'll nod my head in his direction so they'll know who I mean. I'll even point to him, though polite people don't point. Daddy Jack! *Daddy Jack!* They can whistle for him!

Jacob stood over us, smiling softly. The crisp turn of his collar, the top button released, disclosed his velvet, quite dark-colored throat. "Two nice girls," he said. "What have we here?" He picked up my paper.

"Talent!" he said. "Did you do this, honey, by yourself?" He was looking at the cartoon men, not my portrait of Tabby, those tentative strokes in the corner of the page; not at the tilt of her jaw, like a note in music. "Hey, Jack," he said, "now this is good, I can't believe it at her young age." I whispered, "I am nine," as if I wanted to alert him to the true state of affairs. Jacob waved the paper around, delighted. "I could well say this is a prodigy," he said. I turned my face away. It seemed indecent to look at him. In that one moment it seemed to me that the world was blighted, and that every adult throat bubbled, like a garbage pail in August, with the syrup of rotting lies.

I SEE THEM, now, from the car window, children any day, on any road; children going somewhere, disconnected from the routes of adult intent. You see them in twos or threes, in unlikely combinations, sometimes a pair with a little one tagging along, sometimes a boy with two girls. They carry, it might be, a plastic bag with something secret inside, or a stick or box, but no obvious plaything; sometimes a ratty dog processes behind them. Their faces are intent and their missions hidden from adult eyes; they have a geography of their own, urban or rural, that has nothing to do with the milestones and markers that adults use. The country through which they move is older, more intimate than ours. They have their private knowledge of it. You do not expect this knowledge to fail.

There was no need to ask if we were best friends, me and Tabby, as we walked the narrow muddy path by the water. Perhaps it was a canal, but a canal was not a thing I'd seen, and it seemed to me more like a placid inland stream, silver-gray in color, tideless though not motionless, fringed by sedge and tall grasses. My fingers were safely held in the pad of Tabby's palm, and there was a curve of light on the narrow back of her hand. She was a head taller than me, willowy, cool to the touch, even at the hot end of this hot afternoon. She was ten and a quarter years old, she said; lightly, almost as if it were something to shrug away. In her free hand she held a paper bag, and in this bag—which she had taken from her satchel, her eyes modestly downcast—were ripe plums.

They were—in their perfect dumpling under my fingertips, in their cold purple blush—so fleshy that to notch your teeth against their skin seemed like becoming a teatime cannibal, a vampire for a day. I carried my plum in my palm, caressing it, rolling it like a dispossessed eye, and feeling it grow warm from the heat of my skin. We strolled, so, abstinent; till Tabby pulled at my hand, stopped me, and turned me toward her, as if she wanted a witness. She clenched her hand. She rolled the dark fruit in her fist, her eyes on mine. She raised her fist to her sepia mouth. Her small teeth plunged into ripe flesh. Juice ran down her chin. Casually, she wiped it. She turned her face full to mine, and for the first time I saw her frank smile, her lips parted, the gap between her front teeth. She flicked my wrist lightly, with the back of her fingers; I felt the sting of her nails. "Let's go on the wrecks," she said.

It meant we must scramble through a fence. Through a gap there. I knew it was illicit. I knew no would be said: but then what, this afternoon, did I care for no? Under the wire, through the snag of it, the gap already widened by the hands of forerunners, some of whom must have worn double-thickness woolen double-knit mittens to muffle the scratch against their flesh. Once through the wire, Tabby went, "Whoop!"

Then soon she was bouncing, dancing in the realm of the dead cars. They were above our head to the height of three. Her hands reached out to slap at their rusting doorsills and wings. If there had been glass in their windows, it was strewn now at our feet. Scrapes of car paint showed, fawn, banana, a degraded scarlet. I was giddy, and punched my fingers at metal; it crumbled, I was through it. For that moment only I may have laughed; but I do not think so.

She led me on the paths to the heart of the wrecks. We play here, she said, and towed me on. We stopped for a plum each. We laughed. "Are you too young to write a letter?" she asked. I did not answer. "Have you heard of penfriends? I have one already."

All around us, the scrapyard showed its bones. The wrecks stood clear now, stack on stack, against a declining yellow light. When I looked up they seemed to foreshorten, these carcasses, and bear down on me; gaping windows where faces once looked out, engine cavities where the air was blue, treadless tires, wheel arches gaping, trunks unsprung and empty of bags, unraveling springs where seats had been; and some wrecks were warped, reduced as if by fire, bl°°kened. We walked, somber, cheeks bulging, down the paths between. When we had penetrated many rows in, by blind corners, by the swerves enforced on us by the squishy corrosion of the sliding piles, I wanted to ask, why do you play here and who do you mean by *we*, can I be one of your friends or will you forget me, and also can we go now please?

Tabby ducked out of sight, around some rotting heap. I heard her giggle. "Got you!" I said. "Yes!"

She ducked, shying away, but my plum stone hit her square on the temple, and as it touched her flesh I tasted the seducing poison which, if you crack a plum stone, your tongue can feel. Then Tabby broke into a trot, and I chased her: when she skidded to a halt, her flat brown sandals making brakes for her, I stopped too, and glanced up, and saw we had come to a place where I could hardly see the sky. Have a plum, she said. She held the bag out. I am lost, she said. We are, we are, lost. I'm afraid to say.

What came next I cannot, you understand, describe in clock-time. I have never been lost since, not utterly lost, without the sanctuary of sense; without the reasonable hope that I will and can and deserve to be saved. But for that next buried hour, which seemed like a day, and a day with fading light, we ran like rabbits: pile to pile, scrap to scrap, the wrecks towering, as we went deeper, for twenty feet above our heads. I could not blame her. I did not. But I did not see how I could help us either.

If it had been the moors, some ancestral virtue would have propelled me, I felt, toward the metaled road, toward a streambed or cloud that would have conveyed me, soaked and beaten, toward the A57, toward the sanctuary of some stranger's car; and the wet inner breath of that vehicle would have felt to me, whoever owned it, like the wet protective breathing of the belly of the whale. But here, there was nothing alive. There was nothing I could do, for there was nothing natural. The metal stretched, friable, bl°°k, against evening light. We shall have to live on plums forever, I thought. For I had the sense to realize that the only incursion here would be from the wreckers' ball. No flesh would be salvaged here; there would be no rescue team. When Tabby reached for my hand, her fingertips were cold as ball bearings. Once, she heard people calling. Men's voices. She said she did. I heard only distant, formless shouts. They are calling our names, she said. Uncle Jacob, Daddy Jack. They are calling for us.

She began to move, for the first time, in a purposive direction. "Uncle Jacob!" she called. In her eyes was that shifty light of unconviction that I had seen on my mother's face—could it be only this morning? "Uncle Jacob!" She paused in her calling, respectful, so I could call in my turn. But I did not call. I would not, or I could not? A scalding pair of tears popped into my eyes. To know that I lived, I touched the knotted mass of hair, the secret above my nape: my fingers rubbed and rubbed it, round and round. If I survived, it would have to be combed out, with torture. This seemed to militate against life; and then

I felt, for the first time and not the last, that death at least is straightforward. Tabby called, "Uncle Jacob!" She stopped, her breath tight and short, and held out to me the last plum stone, the kernel, sucked clear of flesh.

I took it without disgust from her hand. Tabby's troubled eyes looked at it. It sat in my palm, a shriveled brain from some small animal. Tabby leaned forward. She was still breathing hard. The edge of her littlest nail picked at the convolutions. She put her hand against her ribs. She said, "It is like the map of the world."

There was an interval of praying. I will not disguise it. It was she who raised the prospect. "I know a prayer," she said. I waited. "Little Jesus, meek and mild . . ."

I said, "What's the good of praying to a baby?"

She threw her head back. Her nostrils flared. Prayers began to run out of her.

"Now I lay me down to sleep,

I pray the Lord my soul to keep—"

Stop, I said.

"If I should die before I wake—"

My fist, before I even knew it, clipped her across the mouth.

After a time, she raised her hand there. A fingertip

trembled against the corner of her lip, the crushed flesh like velvet. She crept her lip downward, so that for a moment the inner membrane showed, dark and bruised. There was no blood.

I said, "Aren't you going to cry?"

She said, "Are you?"

I couldn't say, I never cry. It was not true. She knew it. She said softly, it is all right if you want to cry. You're a Catholic, aren't you? Don't you know a Catholic prayer?

Hail Mary, I said. She said, teach it to me. And I could see why: because night was falling: because the sun lay in angry streaks across farther peaks of the junkyard. "Don't you have a watch?" she whispered. "I have one it is Timex, but it is at home, in my bedroom." I said, I have a watch it is Westclox, but I am not allowed to wind it, it is only to be wound by Jack. I wanted to say, and often he is tired, it is late, my watch is winding down, it is stopping but I dare not ask, and when next day it's stopped there's bellowing, only I can do a bleeding thing in this bleeding house. (Door slam.)

There is a certain prayer which never fails. It is to St. Bernard; or by him, I was never quite clear. Remember oh most loving Virgin Mary, that it is a thing *unheard of* that anyone *ever* beseeched thy aid, craved thy intercession or implored thy help and was left forsaken. I thought that I had it, close enough—they might not be the exact words but could a few errors matter, when you were kicking at the very gate of the Immaculate herself? I was ready to implore, ready to crave: and this prayer, I knew, was the best and most powerful prayer ever invented. It was a clear declaration that heaven must help you, or go to hell! It was a taunt, a challenge, to Holy Mary, Mother of God. Get it fixed! Do it now! It is a thing *unheard* of! But just as I was about to begin, I realized I must not say it after all. Because if it didn't work . . .

The strength seemed to drain away then, from my arms and legs. I sat down, in the deep shadows of the wrecks, when all the indications were that we should keep climbing. I wasn't about to take a bet on St. Bernard's prayer, and live my whole life knowing it was useless. My life might be long, it might be very long. I must have thought there were worse circumstances, in which I'd need to deal this final card from my sleeve.

"Climb!" said Tabby. I climbed. I knew—did she?—that the rust might crumble beneath us and drop us into the heart of the wrecks. Climb, she said, and I did: each step tested, so that I learned the resistance of rotting metal, the play and the give beneath my feet, the pathetic cough and wheeze of it, its abandonment and mineral despair. Tabby climbed. Her feet scurried, light, skipping, the soles of her sandals skittering and scratching like rats. And then, like stout Cortez, she stopped, pointed, and stared. "The woodpiles!" I gazed upward into her face. She swayed and teetered, six feet above me. Evening breeze whipped her skirt around her stick legs. "The woodpiles!" Her face opened like a flower.

What she said meant nothing to me, but I understood the message. We are out! she cried. Her arm beckoned me. Come on, come on! She was shouting down to me, but I was crying too hard to hear. I worked myself up beside her: crab arms, crab legs, two steps sideways for every step forward. She reached down and scooped at my arm, catching at my clothes, pulling, hauling me up beside her. I shook myself free. I pulled out the stretched sleeve of my cardigan, eased the shape into the wool, and slid it back past my wrist. I saw the light on the still body of water, and the small muddy path that had brought us there.

"WELL, YOU GIRLS," Jacob said, "don't you know we came calling? Didn't you hear us?"

Well, suppose I did, I thought. Suppose she was right. I can just hear myself, can't you, bawling, here,

Daddy Jack, here I am! Come and save me, Daddy Jack!

It was seven o'clock. They had been composing sandwiches and Jacob had been for ice cream and wafers. Though missed, we had never been a crisis. The main point was that we should be there for the right food at the right time.

The little boys slept on the way home, and I suppose so did I. The next day, next week, next months are lost to me. It startles me now that I can't imagine how I said goodbye to Tabby, and that I can't even remember at what point in the evening she melted away, her crayons in her satchel and her memories in her head. Somehow, with good fortune on our side for once, my family must have rolled home; and it would be another few years before we ventured so far again.

THE FEAR OF being lost comes low these days on the scale of fears I have to live with. I try not to think about my soul, lost or not (though it must be thirty years since my last confession), and I don't generally have to resort to that covert shuffle whereby some women turn the map upside down to count off the road junctions. They say that females can't read maps and never know where they are, but in the year 2000 the Ordnance Survey appointed its first woman director, so I suppose that particular slander loses its force. I married a man who casts a professional eye on the lie of the land, and would prefer me to direct with reference to tumuli, streambeds and ancient monuments. But a finger tracing the major routes is enough for me, and I just say nervously, "We are about two miles from our turnoff or maybe, of course, we are not." Because they are always tearing up the contour lines, plowing under the map, playing hell with the cartography that last year you were sold as *le dernier cri.*

As for the moorland landscape, I know now that I have left it far behind. Even those pinching little boys in the backseat share my appreciation of wildflower verges and lush arable acres. It is possible, I imagine, to build a home on firm ground, a home with long views. I don't know what became of Jacob and his family: did I hear they went home to Africa? Of Tabby, I never heard again. But in recent years, since Jack has been wandering in the country of the dead, I see again his brown skin, his roving caramel eyes, his fretting rage against power and its abuses: and I think perhaps that he was lost all his life, and looking for a house of justice, a place of safety to take him in.

In the short term, though, we continued to live in one of those houses where there was never any money, and doors were slammed hard. One day the glass did spring out of the kitchen cupboard, at the mere touch of my fingertips. At once I threw up my hands, to protect my eyes. Between my fingers, for some years, you could see the delicate scars, like the ghosts of lace gloves, that the cuts left behind.

Learning to Talk

bird tables. They had family cars, known as "little runabouts." At dinnertime they had their lunch, and at teatime they had their dinner. They cleaned themselves up in things called bahthrums.

It was 1963. People were very snobbish, though perhaps not more than they are now. Later, by the time I went to London, certain provincial accents had become acceptable and even smart, but those of my part of the northwest were not among them. The late sixties were an age of equality and people were not supposed to worry about their accents, but they did worry, and tried to adapt their voices—otherwise they found themselves treated with a conscious cheeriness, as if they were bereaved or slightly deformed. When I started at my new school I didn't know that I would become a source of mirth. Groups of girls would approach me with idiot questions, their object being to get me to pronounce certain words, shibboleths; then they would prance off, hooting and giggling.

By the time I was thirteen I had modified my accent to a degree, and my voice itself had brought me a certain notoriety. I was afraid of almost everything, except speaking in public. I had never experienced the sick numbing distress of stage fright, and also, I liked arguing. I might have done well as a shop steward in some particularly noisy factory, but you were not offered these opportunities at our annual Careers Evening. People thought I ought to be a lawyer. So I was sent to Miss Webster, to learn to talk properly.

Miss Webster was not just an elocution teacher; she was also a shopkeeper. Her shop, a few minutes' walk from school, was called Gwen & Marjorie. It sold wool and baby clothes. Miss Webster was Gwen. Marjorie was a stout woman; she moved slowly between the hanks, behind a glass counter. She wore a big cardigan, perhaps of her own composition. In wire racks the knitting-pattern models circulated, their perfect teeth always on display: svelte ladies in lacy-knit boleros, and clean-jawed gents in cable-stitch sweaters. Miss Webster had a plate by the front door, displaying her professional qualifications. At four o'clock the front door was left ajar, so that her pupils from the two local schools could pass without disturbing Marjorie down the corridor at the back of the shop and into the living room where the elocution was performed.

This room overlooked a square of garden, in which a few shrubs withered gently; a scudding, northern late-afternoon sky rushed overhead, and the gas fire flickered and popped. Children—there would be six or seven, all at different stages of their own lessons—would perch on the arms of chairs, and blow their noses, and the convent girls would have to find a corner to stack up their schoolbags and their velour hats. There were no boys. If they didn't talk proper, they had, I suppose, other ways of getting on in life.

Miss Webster was a little sparrowlike woman with a frizz of white hair, prominent shinbones and upswept glasses. It is almost true that you can never be too rich or too thin, but Miss Webster was too thin, and I thought so even though I was thin myself, and even though in those years it was becoming fashionable to look like an habitué of the Capulets' monument. She had only one lung, she used to tell people, and her voice was correspondingly unimpressive. Her accent was precariously genteel, Mancunian with icing. She had been an actress in northern repertory companies. When? How long ago? "I was playing Lady Macbeth at Oldham when Dora Bryan was sweeping the stage."

It was Miss Webster's business to teach us to recite poetry and passages from Shakespeare: to teach us about meter and verse forms, and the mechanics of breathing and articulation; and to enter us for examinations, so that we could get certificates. Most of her pupils had been with her since they were seven or eight, progressing with painful slowness through the various grades. As I was a beginner I was summoned with some of the tots for my first lesson; gloomily Brobdingnagian in my ribbed tights, I read out a little verse about leprechauns which she gave me for a trial run. She said I had better come back with the big girls. There were thirteen-year-olds and thirteen-year-olds, she said, and how could she know in advance which kind I would be? I fancied that as I closed my recitation a perceptible crack appeared in one of the blue glass vases on a shelf above the fireplace. I sat on the floor with my arms around my knees, waiting to be released. Miss Webster handed me a diagram of the respiratory tract: not of hers, of course, but of a more ideal one. Gwen and Marjorie's pet entered the room, a Yorkshire terrier which ran about among our legs and satchels. There was a little pink bow in its topknot, which I transferred mentally to Miss Webster's own head. She and the dog seemed alike: crushable, yappy, not very bright.

Miss Webster, at least, knew how one ought to sound. The weekly exercises were rhymes, incorporating every tricky vowel. Each one of them was a baited trap, laid by the governors of Miss Webster's professional body to ensnare every kind of regional accent:

Father's car is a Jaguar,
And Pa drives rather fast,
Castles, farms and drafty barns,
We go charging past . . .

My brothers and I had often been baffled, when we were first translated to Cheshire. "What do they mean," asked the youngest, now at a Church of England school, "when they talk about the Kingdom, the par and the glory?" And for years I thought you could win a point at tennis with a well-executed parsing shot.

I hadn't been to the south of England yet; it didn't occur to me that I was being taught the provincialisms of another part of the country. Received Pronunciation was the goal, with a distinct southern ring. Somewhere in the West Country perhaps, a schoolgirl like me was tripping over some other set of caltrops:

Roy's employed in Droitwich
In a first-class oyster bar;
Moira tends to linger
As she sips her Noilly Prat . . .

I went to Miss Webster every term-time Tuesday for the next three years. Then after my lessons I would trail home through the darkening streets, passing other wool shops with baby clothes in their windows, and the village delicatessen with its range of pale cold meats, and the posters on the park noticeboard advertising whist drives and bring-and-buy sales. I used to pretend, to alleviate the boredom of the walk, that I was a spy in a foreign country, a woman passing for someone else in a country approaching war, where the goods in the shop windows would be vanishing soon and austerity would be the order of the day; and what fueled my fantasy was the iron bridge over the old canal, and the prewar cut of my school raincoat, and the fatigue on the faces of the commuters who came down the station steps, hurrying home to their through-lounges. When I rushed into the shops before they closed with the list my mother had given me, I pretended that I was obtaining black-market provisions, and that my schoolbag was full of atomic secrets. I don't know why I had this daydream, though I know that the totality of the transformation was not marred by the fact that in my life as a spy I often carried, according to season, my tennis racket or hockey stick. It was a lonely sort of dream, full of ennui and distaste. There should be support groups, like a twelve-step program, for young people who hate being young. Since I was at other people's pieces, were held in Manchester at the Methodist Central Hall. During my years, there were two examiners; you never knew, when you entered the room, which one it would be. The female examiner had a querulous voice, which broke off in the middle of sentences, as if she were too shocked to continue. The male examiner was seventy, or eighty perhaps, or ninety, and he wore a watch chain. He was a florid man, who stared ahead of him, and would sometimes lean forward in his chair, trembling with suppressed effort, as if he had been used to more activity in his life and did not recognize what he had come to. He looked like a man who had seen standards slip.

The ways in which the examination pieces were recited owed nothing to Miss Webster's tuition. It was something the pupils worked out among themselves, with the unseen aid of generations of past pupils. While you were waiting to recite your piece of Shakespeare to Miss Webster, you would be listening to some other pupil who was preparing for the grade above yours. So if a short-winded child took a breath in the wrong place, or introduced through ignorance or boredom some nonsensical inflection, it would be taken up by the others, and become definitive, and hang around for years. I never knew Miss Webster to suggest a phrasing; the truth is, I think, that she didn't understand Shakespeare, and must have learned to play Lady Macbeth by some theatrical equivalent of painting by numbers. She was not responsible for the choice of pieces; those were laid down by the examining council. For one exam—Grade VII, I think—it was necessary to perform the parts of both Oswald and Goneril, skipping about to face oneself, altering one's voice and making, in both directions, the Gesture.

According to Miss Webster, only one gesture was necessary or even permissible when reciting Shakespeare. It was a full sweep of the arm, palm toward the audience; three bottom fingers glued together, thumb raised and almost vertical, and the forefinger bisecting the angle. All passion, all joy, all dismay was reducible to this one gesture; it would do for Titus Andronicus, for Charmian and for Dogberry. I must have been slow, or perhaps incredulous, for Miss Webster herself took my hand in her cold age-spotted hand, and fixed my fingers into this thespian V-sign.

I usually, when I got into the exam room, said my pieces the way I liked, and it must have been that my originality grated on the examiners' ears, because although I did well I never got the very best marks; and I was left, too, with the feeling that I was a hypocrite. I was seventeen when I went to the Central Hall for the last time, to be examined for my diploma. It was November, a cold and very wet morning, and I wore boots, and my school mackintosh, and my navy-blue school skirt and my striped shirt blouse; but I took the liberty of going into the Ladies at Piccadilly station, and letting my hair out of the elastic bands to which the school rules confined it. I brushed it in front of the mirror. It was very long and straight and pale, as I was myself, and the image I presented, turning away from British Rail's speckled glass, was a bizarre one; as if the Lady of Shalott had left the web and left the loom and turned into a traffic warden. The sodden shapes of Mancunians jostled in Oldham Street, and the building, when I scurried into its shelter, smelled of linoleum and Dettol, and thin Methodist prayer.

Miss Webster was waiting for me; anxious, rather blue around the lips. She quailed when she saw my boots. That was not proper dress, she said, the examiner would not like it, I could not go in wearing those boots. I had nothing to say, really. I took off my scarf and laid it over the back of a chair. Candidates for the various grades sat by their teachers, scuffling their feet, their scrubby little hands knotted together in fear. I had already taken my written paper; it had been very easy. Could I go in my stockinged feet, I asked, would that be better? Dim institutional lights burned in white globes. Cars splashed by outside, their headlights on, heading for Oldham Road and the sooty outer suburbs. Puddles of water had formed on the lino under my boots. I kicked them off, and shrank an inch or two. That would certainly not do, Miss Webster said. She would lend me her shoes.

Miss Webster's shoes were two-and-a-half sizes bigger than mine. They were court shoes, of fake crocodile; they had ferocious points in front, and three-and-a-half-inch spike heels. They were, I suppose, the footwear of a retired actress, but I did not grasp the poignancy of the moment. I put my feet into them, and staggered a few paces, clutching at the backs of chairs. Why did I agree to it? I never, in those years, thought in the short term. I had fallen into a habit of acquiescence; I believed that, in the long term, I should make everyone else look a fool.

When my name was called I lurched into the examination room. It was the gentleman. Neither he nor his female colleague had ever attempted to put a candidate at her ease. They were like driving examiners, asking questions but offering no comment, hardly the bare civilities, though the man had once remarked to me gloomily that I had a lisp. Today he looked flushed, and in his usual state of arrested tension, and yet he looked ponderous, and as if he hated the young.

My set piece was an extract from *Henry VIII*. It was lucky I had only one character to play, because if I had tried to maneuver myself about I would have fallen over. I picked my spot, I swayed about on it. I could see myself, the uniform that hung on me, the spot of ink on my cuff, my white child's face, and Miss Webster's mock crocs. I had not known that my performance as Queen Katharine would be most remarkable from the ankle down. It was the speech where Katharine, about to be repudiated, begs the monarch to remember their life together, and in the early stages of my rehearsals I had been unable to get through it without dissolving into tears, and I needed to stop myself crying by an act of will; the examiner would want to hear the verse. I had already decided I would not make the Gesture. If the examiner thought I did not know the Gesture, he would just have to mark me down. There were certain lines that seemed packed with emotion like high explosive; the only way to get through was to deliver the entire speech while thinking of something else.

Already, as I began, the examiner's eyes had slithered down to my body and glued themselves to my feet. "I am a most poor woman, and a stranger / Born out of your dominions . . ." I had somehow slid forward in the shoes, so that my toes were gripped painfully in the points—"having here / No judge indifferent . . ." and I tried to shuffle backward a bit—"Alas, sir, in what have I offended you?" I kept my voice low, the voice of a middle-aged woman, foreign and confused, under great tension and stress; I kept my hands clasped, as if trying to damp down disaster. Then abruptly the examiner lurched forward, and hunched his shoulders, and rose halfway out of his chair to peer fixedly down at my feet. Teetering, quite without intent, another few inches toward him, I tried to press on . . . "What cause / Hath my behavior given to your displeasure / That thus you should proceed to put me off / And take your good grace from me?"

"That will be enough Shakespeare," the examiner said.

But I took a breath, and demanded of him, "When was the hour I ever contradicted your desire?" My ankles ached. I did not know how anyone could walk in these shoes. It was like being on stilts. And why should such a small woman have such very long thin feet? "Sir, call to mind / That I have been your wife, in this obedience . . ." He raised his face, and looked at me wonderingly. And then suddenly, when I reached the line "Upward of twenty years," I was overwhelmed: by the content of the speech, by the mock crocs, by the whole business of learning to talk. I burst noisily into tears, and stood for a long moment, swaying before the examiner, and thinking with longing of those abandoned children who are suckled by wolves and who all their lives remain mute. Surely it was not necessary to talk for a living? Wouldn't it be possible to keep your mouth shut, and perhaps write things down; perhaps write what Miss Webster would call bucks?

I found a handkerchief in the sleeve of my school sweater. The examiner motioned me to a chair. He turned to the papers before him, his eyes carefully downcast, fighting, I could see, his inclination to stare at my shoes. Perhaps afterward he would think it all a dream. He asked me some questions, then; but not the question he wanted to ask. Did I believe, he inquired, that an ability to analyze meter contributed to one's understanding of English poetry? I sniffed, and said, not in the least.

That was my last examination. I gave Miss Webster her shoes back and put on my boots and walked back to the station, red-eyed, in the rain. I knew that a phase of my life was coming to an end and that soon I would be able to get away. A few weeks later I received my diploma, set out in florid scrollwork. My recitations had got me certified. I had letters after my name.

A short time ago I went back home and drove by my school and by Miss Webster's door. Nothing had changed, and yet it had changed. The wool shop was still there, selling shawls and bobble hats. The sign above just says MARJORIE, and the plate has gone from the door. The shops around have come down in the world; the windows are dirty, the paint is peeling. The council houses across the road, once respectable, look seedy now; their walls are pockmarked, as if they had recently been under fire. This small town, which was prosperous, conceited and plump, has lost its prosperity now, and shares in the general decay of the northwest; and by a mysterious process of downward leveling, its vowels have grown broader, and its people more dour, and the weather, I think, is quite possibly colder than it used to be. Moira would not linger there now, to sip her Noilly Prat. The ocean that separated my childhood from my teenage years has dried up: or at least, we are all in the same boat. There is no point in being bitter. Expectations were inflated for a few years, and have now been punctured, and people's lives have become uncomfortable and insecure, and their future has been taken away. All those places where people don't talk proper look curiously alike; driving through the everlasting soft gray blanket of rain, it is possible to imagine oneself in the suburbs of Belfast. I am glad I don't live there, in the nursery of my vowels. I never ironed them out, really. But I know the Gesture; and it is surprising, from time to time, how consoling that can be.

Third Floor Rising

The summer of my eighteenth birthday I had my first job. It was to fill the time between leaving school and going away to university in London. The previous summer I'd been old enough to work, but I had to stay at home and mind the children, while my mother pursued her glittering career.

For most of the years until I was sixteen, my mother had devoted herself to the care of a sick child. First it was me, until I went to senior school. Then I got abruptly better, by an act of will on my mother's part. My high fevers ceased, or ceased to be noticed, or if they were noticed they stopped being interesting. My youngest brother, his struggles for breath and his nighttime cough, was elected to my old place in the household's economy. In my case I had been to school sporadically, but my brother didn't go at all. He played by himself in the garden under a pewter sky, with the fugitive glitter of snow behind it. He lay on his daybed in the room with the television blaring, and turned the pages of a book. One evening we were watching the news when our whole room lit up with a sick white light, and a bolt of ball lightning ripped the lower limbs from the poplar tree and blew the glass from the window frame, whump, fist of God. The shards were strewed over his crocheted blanket, the dog howled, the rain blew into the wreckage of the room and the neighbors squeaked and gibbered in the streets.

A short time after this my mother answered an advertisement for a saleswoman on the fashion floor at Affleck & Brown, which was a small, cramped, old-fashioned department store in Manchester. She had to walk to the station and then travel by train, then walk again to Oldham Street. This was a wonder to me, because I thought she'd given up going out. To do the job she had to have white blouses and black skirts. She bought some at C&A, and this amazed me too, because in our house we got our clothes by less straightforward methods than purchase: by a process of transmogrification, whereby cardigans were unraveled and reappeared as woolen berets and collars were wrenched off to extend hems and what were armholes for the stout became leg holes for the lean. When I was seven I'd had my winter coats made out of two that had belonged to my godmother. Pockets, lapels, everything was miniaturized: except the buttons, which were the originals, and stood out like banqueting plates, or targets for an arrow on my pigeon chest.

My mother had been to school in an age when most people didn't take exams, and she hadn't much to put on her application form. But she got the job, and soon personal disasters began to overtake the people who had appointed her; with them out of the way, she was promoted first to deputy and then to manageress of her department. She developed an airy meringue of white-blond hair, very tall shoes—not just high heels but little boosts under the soles—and an airy way of talking and gesturing; and she began to encourage her staff to lie about their ages, which seemed to suggest she was lying about her own. She came home late and quarrelsome, with something unlikely in her crocodile bag. It might be a bag of crinkle-cut chips, which tasted of grease and air, a pack of frozen beefburgers which, under the grill, bubbled up with oily spots the gray-yellow color of a Manchester smog. In time the chip pan got banned, to save the paintwork and to make a class statement, but by then I was living up the road with my friend

Anne Terese, and what the others got for rations was something I preferred not to think about.

When I was seventeen I was as unprepared for life as if I had spent my childhood on a mountainside minding goats. I was given to contemplation of nature, strolling about in the woods and fields. I was given to going to Stockport library and getting seven big books at a time about Latin American revolutions; waiting for an hour in the rain for the bus home, shifting the books at my feet and sometimes picking them up in expectation of a bus and cradling them in my arms, relishing their public dirt-edged pages, and the anticipation of finding inside them urgent notes from small-town obsessives: "NOT Guatemala!!!!" penciled in the margin, or rather incised into the page with a stub of graphite and the cedar's ragged edge. In our house, too, we never had a pencil sharpener. If you wanted a point you went to my mother and she held the pencil in her fist and swiped chunks off it with the bread knife.

It wasn't the fault of my education that I was so unworldly, because most of my contemporaries were normal, for their time and place and class. But they seemed to be made of a denser, plusher substance than myself. You could imagine them being women, and having upholstery and airing cupboards.

There was air in the spaces between my bones, smoke between my ribs. Pavements hurt my feet. Salt sought out ulcers in my tongue. I was given to prodigious vomiting for no reason. I was cold when I woke up and I thought I would go on being it, always. So later, when I was twenty-four and I was offered a chance to migrate to the tropics, I seized on it because I thought now, now at least I will never be cold again.

My holiday job was secured before the interview; who, at Affleck & Brown, would have turned down the daughter of my ever-popular mother? But it was a formality: the mild personnel officer in his dun-colored suit, in a back office so brown that I thought I had never seen the color before, in every variety of tobacco spit and jaundice, every texture of Bakelite and Formica. Here I entered, fresh as 1970 in my little cotton shift, and here I was drawn backward to the fifties, to the brown world of the National Insurance Card, and the yellowed notice from the Wages Council peeling from the distempered wall. Here I was wished luck and walked out on to the carpet, into the public world. "Draws your feet, this carpet," said a voice from between the rails.

It came from a shuddering white face, from wagging jowls, from a slow rolling mass of flesh, fiercely corseted inside a dress of stretched black polyester:

corseted into the shape of a bulbous flower vase, and the skin with the murky sheen of carnation water two days old. Reek of armpits, rattling cough; these were my colleagues. Life in the stores had destroyed them. They had chronic sniffles from the dust and bladder infections from the dirty lavatories. Their veins bulged through elastic stockings. They lived on £15 per week. They didn't work on commission, so they never sold anything if they could help it. Their rheumy malice drove customers back to the escalators and down into the street.

The personnel officer set me to work in the department next to my mother. I was able to study her in action, wafting across the floor in whatever creation she was wearing that day; she was no longer in subfusc, but picked her garments from her own stock. She had developed a manner that was gracious, not to say condescending, combined with a tip-tilted flirtatiousness that she tried out on the wilting gays who were almost the only men in the store; she was liked by her staff—her girls, as she called them—for her prettiness and high spirits.

They didn't seem, the girls, quite so decrepit as the ones who worked for my department, although I soon found out that they had a variety of intractable personal problems, which were meat and drink to my mother, which were in fact what she had instead of meat and drink, because now it was her role in life to stay a size 10, pretend she was a size 8, and so set an example to womankind. The girls had divorces, bad debts, vitamin deficiencies, premenstrual tension, and children with fits and deformities. Their houses were given to subsidence and collapse, floods and molds, and it seemed to me that they specialized in obsolescent diseases such as smallpox or conditions such as scrapie that only a few morbid-minded people like me had heard of in those days. The worse off they were, the more disorderly and hopeless their lives, the more my mother doted on them. Even today, thirty years on, many of them keep in touch with her. "Mrs. D rang," she will say. "The IRA have bombed her house again and her daughter's been engulfed in a tidal wave, but she asked to be remembered to you." At Christmas, and on the occasions of her falsified birthdays, these girls would buy my mother colored-glass ornaments, and adjuncts to the good life, like soda siphons. They were inner-city women with flat Manchester voices, but my mother and the other department heads talked in peculiar purse-lipped ways designed not to let their vowels show.

I was not employed by the store itself, but by a "shop-in-shop" called English Lady. There were women, tending to the elderly, who wanted what it offered: dress-and-coat ensembles that I called wedding uniforms, summer frocks and "separates" in artificial fabrics and pastel shades, washable and easy-iron. In those days people still went out in April to buy a summer coat of pink showerproof poplin, or a light wool with a shadow check, and they bought blazers, boleros and blouses, and trouser ensembles with long tunic tops under which they wore stockings and suspenders, the bumps of the suspenders showing through the polyester. In winter English Lady specialized in camel coats, which their wearers dutifully renewed every few years, expecting exactly the same style and getting it. There were also—for the winter stock was coming in, long before I left for London—coats called llamas, which were an unhealthy silver-gray, and shaggy, like hair shirts turned out, but hair shirts with pockets. For the autumn also there were bristling tweeds, and lumpen stinking sheepskins which we chained to the rails, because English Lady feared for their safety. Herding them was heavy work; they exhaled with a grunt when they were touched, and jostled for lebensraum, puffing out their bulk and testing their bonds inch by squeaky inch.

Customers were scarce that summer. Once the morning dusting was over and we had done the day's updates on varicose veins, there was a desert of time to be got through: days of stupefying heat, thirst and boredom, with no air, no natural light, only a dim fluorescence above which gave a corpse-tint to the freshest skins. Sometimes as I stood I thought furiously about the French Revolution, which had come to preoccupy me. Sometimes my mother tripped across the carpet, fluttering her fingers at me, smiling upon her workforce.

My own boss was called Daphne. She wore goggle-sized fashion specs with colored rims, behind which swam void pale eyes. In theory she and my mother were friends, but I soon realized, with a sense of shock, that among her peers my mother was a target for envy, and would have been secretly sabotaged if the other bosses had been bright enough to think how to do it. Daphne worked me relentlessly during those summer weeks, finding for me tasks that no one had done in years: cleaning in the stockrooms that were mice-ridden and thick with dust, boxing up great consignments of wire hangers which leaped from their bundles to claw at my arms like rats breaking out of a pet shop. The northwest was filthy in those days, and the rooms behind the scenes at Affleck & Brown were a dark and secret aspect of the filth. The feet-drawing carpets, the thick polythene in which the clothes came swathed, the neglected warp and weft of those garments that failed to sell and were bastilled in distant stockrooms: all these attracted a nap of sticky fluff which magnetized the particles of the Manchester atmosphere, which coated the hands and streaked the face, so that I must often have looked less like a "junior sales" than a scab in a pit strike, my eyes traveling suspiciously when I surfaced, my hands contaminated, held away from my body in a gesture designed both to placate and ward off.

Sometimes, behind some packed rail draped in yellowing calico, behind some pile of boxes whose labels were faded to illegibility, I could sense a movement, a kind of shifting of feet, a murmur: "Mrs. Solomons?" I would call. "Mrs. Segal?" No answer: just the whispered exhalation of worsted and mohair: the deep intestinal creak of suede and leather: the faint squeal of unoiled metal wheels. Perhaps it was Daphne, spying on me? But sometimes at five thirty when the fitting rooms had to be cleared, I would come across a closed curtain at the end of a row, and I would turn and walk away without pulling it back, afflicted by sudden shyness or by fear of seeing something that I shouldn't see. It is easy to imagine that hanging fabric is bulked out by flesh, or that stitch and seam rehearse, after hours, a human shape without bones.

My colleagues, breathing over me the faint minted aroma of their indigestion remedies, received me with unbounded kindness. My pallor attracted their tut-tutting sanction, and caused them to recommend the red meat that never passed their own lips. Perhaps my remoteness alarmed them, as I stood entranced among the edge-to-edge jackets; and then I would snap back and sell something, which alarmed them too. I liked the challenge of suiting the garments to the women who wanted them, of making a fit, of gratifying harmless desire. I liked tearing off the tickets from the frocks as they were sold, and looping a carrier bag considerately around an arthritic wrist. Sometimes the elderly customers would try to give me tips, which upset me. "I don't come often now," said one twisted, gracious old person. "But when I do come, I always give."

At the end of each working day my mother and I winced arm in arm to Piccadilly station, up the hill from Market Street, past the hot cafés stewing with grease and the NHS clinic that was always advertising for people to step in and donate blood. (I stepped in as soon as I was eighteen, but they turned me around and stepped me straight back out again.) It seemed to me that my job amounted to standing up for a living, and that no one should have to do it: standing hour after hour, standing when there was no customer in sight, standing in the fuggy heat from nine in the morning till five thirty at night with an hour for lunch in which you sprang out of the building and walked, gulping in the air. You stood long after your feet throbbed and your calves ached, and the ache wasn't gone by next morning when the standing started again. Maybe my mother was better off than me, because she had a tiny shelf of an office to sit in, a chair to perch on. But then she had her shoes, much more pernicious than my small suede sandals; her whole existence was much more high.

Some nights, maybe twice in the week, there were problems with the trains. Once there was an hour's delay. Hunger made us buoyant: talking gaily of the many catastrophes that had beset my mother's girls that day, we nibbled at a green apple she had produced from her bag, turn and turn about. We were not angry or guilty about being late because there was nothing we could do, and our mood was innocent, blithe, until we found ourselves penned up in the hall of our little house with my stepfather snarling. Our giggling stopped: what I have often remarked as brutal is the side of the human hand, tensed, wedge-like, ready to strike like an axe. Something then occurred. I'm not clear what it was. It isn't true that if you're very angry it gives you strength. If you're very angry it gives you a swimming head and limbs weak at the joints, but you do it anyway, a thing you've never done before, you speak the curse, you move, you pin against the wall, you say a certain death formula and what you say you mean; the effect is in proportion to the shock, as if the Meek had got out from the Sermon on the Mount and raked the crossroads with machine-gun fire.

After this, for a while, I left home. My mother and I parted every evening at the end of our road. She was more in sorrow than in anger, but sometimes she was in anger; I realize now that my intervention had interrupted some marital game of hers. When we drew near the end of our day's journey she'd stop chattering about the girls, and she'd move—reluctantly, I often felt—into some remote sniffy territory, putting deliberate distance between us. I would labor on up the hill to where I'd moved in with Anne Terese. She was now alone in the family house. Her parents had parted that summer, and perhaps they hadn't got the hang of it; instead of one going and one staying, both of them had walked out. We didn't compare our families much; we tried on the clothes in the wardrobes, and rearranged the furniture. The house was a peculiar one, prefabricated, contingent but homely, with a stove in the sitting room, and a deep enamel sink, and none of the appliances, like fridges, that people took for granted in the year 1970.

Anne Terese was working for the summer at a factory that made rubber-soled slippers. The work was hard, but every part of her body was hard and efficient too. In the evening, while I sagged feebly on a kitchen chair, she breaded cutlets, and sliced tomato and cucumber on to a glass dish. She made a Polish cake that was heavy with eggs and ripe cherries. At dusk we sat on the porch, in the faint blown scent of old roses. Hope, fine as cobwebs, draped our bare arms and floated across our shoulders, each strand shivering with twilit blue. When the moon rose we moved indoors to our beds, still sleepily murmuring. Anne Terese thought six children would suit her. I thought it would be good if I could stop vomiting.

Sometimes, as I wandered the floor at English Lady, I'd pretend that I was a supervisor at a refugee camp and that the frocks were the inhabitants. When I packed one and threw its ticket into a box I said to myself that I'd resettled it.

Each day began and ended with the count. You

took a piece of paper and ruled it into columns for the different types of stock, so that you didn't get the two-pieces mixed up with the Dress & Jackets, even though they were two pieces also. You had to make categories for the garments that had no name, like the bifurcated items that head office had sent several seasons ago; made of hairy gray-blue tweed, they were some kind of flying suit perhaps, of a kind to be worn by Biggles's nanny. When the sales came around, Daphne would always reduce them, but they remained on the rails, their stiff arms thrust out and their legs wrapped around their necks to keep them from trailing on the carpet.

When you had made your categories you went between the rails and counted, and it was always wrong. You would then patrol the floor looking for English Ladies that had tucked themselves in among the Eastex or Windsmoor. You would haul them back by their necks and thrust them on the rails. But, while it was easy to see why the count should be wrong after the working day, it was less easy to understand why the stock should move around at night. "Spooks," I said robustly. I thought they must come down from the third-floor bedding (the sheeted dead) and try on our garments, hissing with spooky excitement, and sliding their phantom limbs into legs and sleeves.

I passed the summer so, in talking to tramps in Piccadilly Gardens; in buying ripe strawberries from the barrows for my lunch; in cooling my forehead against the gunmetal grille of the door of the goods lift. When Daphne castigated me for this failing and that, I would sigh will-do-better, but later I would aim secret kicks at the flying suits, and torture them by wrapping their legs more tightly around their necks and knotting them behind the hanger. To Daphne's face, I was compliance itself. I didn't want my mother to incur even more rancid female hatred, which would snarl invisible about her trim ankles, snag her kitten heels when I was long gone and marching through London streets.

But then, as September approached, I found that the whole subject of the count was making me restless. Each evening we could only square it with the stock sheets by writing "15 in back" at the end of the Dress & Jackets column, and it occurred to me that in all my groveling and delving I'd never run across these oddments. "You know," I said to Daphne, "where we always write '15 in back'? Where are they?"

"In back," said Daphne. We were in her office, a scant wedge shape partitioned off from the sales floor.

"But where?" I said. "I've never seen them."

Daphne slotted a cigarette into her mouth. With one hand she flipped a page of a stock list, in the other hovered a dribbling ballpoint pen. A thin plume of smoke leaked from her lips. "Don't you smoke yet?" she said. "Aren't you tempted?"

I had wondered, a time or two, why people try to trap you into new vices. Ours was a home that was militantly anti-tobacco. "I haven't thought about it really . . . I don't suppose . . . Well, if your parents don't smoke . . . I couldn't at home anyway, it would be very bad for my brother."

Daphne stared at me. A little hoot issued from her, like a hiccup, and then a derisive shout of laughter. "What! Your mother smokes like a chimney! Every break! Every lunchtime! Haven't you seen her? You must have seen her!"

"No," I said. "I have never." I was the more deceived.

A gobbet of ink dropped from Daphne's pen. "Have I spoken out of turn?"

"That's all right," I said.

I told myself I welcomed information, information from any source.

Daphne looked at me glassily. "Anyway," she said, "why should it be bad for your brother?"

I looked at my watch. "Mrs. Segal's lunch." I smiled. I headed back to the sales floor. I said to myself, it can't matter. Tiny household lies. Pragmatic lies. Amusing, probably: given time. Trivial: like a needle-point snapped under the skin.

But later that afternoon, I sought the 15 in back. I tunneled my way into lightless holes, where my toes were stubbed by bulging rotten boxes of unknown provenance. The cartons I had made myself, and bound with twine, had never been dispatched by Daphne, but left to squat in collapsing stacks. Now the wire hangers nipped at my calves as they worked their way out. Levering aside the bulky winter stock, thwacking the llamas away from me, I burrowed my way to the farthest corner. Give me that mattock and the wrenching iron.

Nothing. I named every garment I saw, scrabbling inside their shrouds: lifting them by their collars to peep at their labels, or, if I could not lift them, shredding their plastic frills into ruffs around their throats. I saw labels and I saw things that might have been Dress & Jackets but I did not see Dress & Jackets with the label I wanted. The 15 were nowhere to be found. I fought my way back to the air. I never looked back. I scratched it on my pad: zero, nix, nought. Diddly-squat, as the men said. Dress & Jackets, nil. If they had ever been known to exist, they didn't now. I saw how it was; they were to be conjured into being, the 15, to cover a mighty embarrassment, some awesome negligence or theft that had knocked the count to its knees gibbering. They were a fiction, perhaps an antique one; perhaps even older than Daphne. They were an adjustment to reality. They were a tale told by an idiot: to which I had added a phrase or two.

I reemerged on to the floor. It was three o'clock. One of those dead afternoons, adumbrated, slumberous: not a customer in view. Limp from lack of regard, the stock hung like rags. A long mirror showed a dark smudge across my cheek. My sandals were coated with poisoned grime. I limped to the battered bureau where we kept our duplicate books and spare buttons, and took a duster out of the drawer. I rolled it up and brushed myself down, then moved out on to the floor, between the rails, and dusted between the garments: parting the hangers and polishing the steel spaces between. Somehow the afternoon passed. That night I declined to write "15 in back" at the end of the count: until my colleagues became too upset to bear, and one showed signs of hyperventilating. So in the end I did consent to write the phrase, but I wrote it quite faintly in pencil, with a question mark after it that was fainter still.

When the new school term began, it emerged that there was nothing wrong with my brother anymore. He was eleven now, quite fit enough to go to high school. We digested this surprising fact, but no one was quite as glad about it as they should have been. Within months my mother was headhunted, her services sought by mackintosh purveyors and knitwear concessions; she had her pick of jobs, and moved to bigger stores, becoming blonder year by year, rising like a champagne bubble, to command larger numbers of girls and bigger counts and attract even more animosity and spite. At home she pursued her impromptu housekeeping, scouring the bath with powder meant for the washing machine and, when the washing machine broke down, throwing a tablecloth over it and using it as a sort of sideboard while she trained my siblings to go to the launderette.

A few years later Affleck closed, and the whole district around it went to seed. It was taken over by pornographers, and those kinds of traders who sell plastic laundry baskets, dodgy electric fires and molded Christmas novelties such as bouncing mince pies and whistling seraphim. The building itself was leased by a high-street clothing store, who traded briefly from its crumbling shell. I was long gone, of course, but I kept friends in the north, and had in my chain of acquaintances a Saturday girl who worked for the new occupiers. They only used the lower floors; from the second floor upward, the building had been sealed. The fire doors had been closed and locked shut, the escalators had been removed, and the back staircases now ended in blind walls. But the staff were disturbed, said the Saturday girl, by noises from the bricked-in cavity above their heads: by footsteps, and by the sound of a woman screaming.

When I heard this I felt cold and felt sickness in the pit of my stomach, because I knew it was a true ghost story, as true as these things go. It had been no dizzy imp that came down from above and pulled buttons off the frocks, or walked them across the floor and mixed them in with the Jaeger. It was something staler, heavier, grossly sinister and perverse. But I only knew this in retrospect. When I looked back from, say, the age of twenty-three to the age of eighteen, I realized that, in those years, everything had been far worse than it seemed at the time.

The Clean Slate

About eleven o'clock this morning—after the nurses had "tidied her up" as they put it, and she'd fixed her eye makeup—I sat down by my mother's bed and coaxed her to do the family tree with me. Considering how self-centered she is, it worked out surprisingly well. She would like to write "VERONICA" in the center of the paper and strike lines of force running outward from herself. But (although she thinks this would give you an accurate picture of the world) she does have a grasp on how these things are done. She has seen the genealogy of the Kings and Queens of England, their spurious portraits glowing by their names, stamp-sized and in stained-glass colors; their plaits of flaxen hair, their crude medieval crowns with gems like sucked sweets.

She has seen these, in the books she pretends to

read. So she understands that you can also do a family tree for us, the poor bloody infantry.

The pictures by the names will be equally spurious. A woman once told me that there was no family so poor, when the last century ended, that they didn't have their photographs taken. It might be true. In that case, somebody burned ours.

I BEGAN THIS enterprise because I wanted to find out something about my ancestors who lived in the drowned village. I thought it might provide a reason for my fear of water—one I could use to make people feel bad, when they advise me that swimming is good exercise for a person of my age. Then again, I thought it might be a topic I could turn into cash. I could go to Dunwich, I thought, and write about a village that slipped into the sea. Or to Norfolk, to talk to people who have mortgaged houses on the edge of cliffs. I could work it up into a feature for the Sunday press. They could send a photographer, and we could balance on the cliff edge at Overstrand, just one rusting wire between us and infinite blue light.

But Veronica was not interested in the submerged. She twitched at the ribbons at her bosom—still firm, by the way—and eased herself irritably against the pillows. The veins in her hands stood out, as if she had sapphires and wore them beneath the skin. She hardly listened to my questions, and said in a huffy way, "I really can't tell you much about all that, I'm afraid."

The people from the drowned village were on her father's side of the family, and were English. Veronica was interested in matriarchies, in Irish matriarchies, and in reliving great moments in the life of matriarchies by repeating the same old stories: the jokes that have lost their punch lines, the retorts and witty snubs that have come unfastened from their origins. Perhaps I shouldn't blame her, but I do. I distrust anecdote. I like to understand history through figures and percentages of these figures, through knowing the price of coal and the price of corn, and the price of a loaf in Paris on the day the Bastille fell. I like to be free, so far as I can, from the tyranny of interpretation.

THE VILLAGE OF Derwent began to sink beneath the water in the winter of 1943. This was years before I was born. The young Veronica was no doubt forming up thoughts of what children she would have, and how she would make them turn out. She had white skin and green eyes and dyed her hair red with patent formulations. It didn't really matter what man she married, he was only a vehicle for her dynastic ambitions.

Veronica's mother—my maternal grandmother—was called Agnes. She came from a family of twelve. Don't worry, I won't give you a rundown on each one of them. I couldn't, if I wanted to. When I ask Veronica to help me fill in the gaps, she obliges with some story that relates to herself, and then hints—if I try to bring her back to the subject—that there are some things best left unsaid. "There was more to that episode than was ever divulged," she would say. I did find out a few facts about the previous generation: none of them cheerful. That one brother went to prison (willingly) for a theft committed by another. That one sister had a child who died unchristened within minutes of birth. She was a daughter whose existence flickered briefly somewhere between the wars; she has no name, and her younger brother to this very day does not know of her existence. Not really a person: more like a negative that was never developed.

THE VILLAGE OF Derwent didn't die of an accident, but of a policy. Water was needed by the urban populations of Manchester, Sheffield, Nottingham and Leicester. And so in 1935 they began to build a dam across the River Derwent. Ladybower was the dam's name.

When Derwent was flooded it was already flattened, already deserted. But when I was a child I didn't know this. I understood that the people themselves had left before the flood, but I imagined them going about their daily work till the last possible moment: listening out for a warning, something like an air-raid siren, and then immediately dropping whatever it was they were doing. I saw them shrugging into their stout woolen coats—buttoning in the children, tickling smiling chins—and picking up small suitcases and brown paper parcels, trudging with resigned Derbyshire faces to meeting points on the corner. I saw them laying down their knitting in mid-stitch, throwing a peapod half shelled into the colander: folding away the morning paper with a phrase half read, an ellipsis that would last their lifetimes.

"LEICESTER, DID YOU say?" Veronica beamed at me. "Your uncle Finbar was last seen in Leicester. He had a market stall."

I shuffled my hospital armchair forward, across the BUPA contract carpet. "Your uncle," I said. "That's my great-uncle."

"Yes." She can't think why I quibble: what's hers is mine.

"What was he selling?"

"Old clothes." Veronica chuckled knowingly. "So it was said."

I didn't rise to her bait. All I want from her is some dates. She likes to make mysteries and imply she has secret knowledge. She won't say which year she was born and has told a blatant lie about her age to the admissions people, which could of course jeopardize her insurance claim. Also, I am conjoined to the same insurance scheme, and they might begin to wonder about me if they ever compare files and see that by their records my mother is only ten years older than me.

A man once told me that you can date women by looking at the backs of their knees. That delta of soft flesh and broken veins, he swore, it is the only thing that cannot lie.

"They were a wild lot," Veronica said. "Your uncles. They were," she said, "you must remember, Irishmen."

No, they weren't. Irish, yes, I concede. But not wild, not nearly wild enough. They drank when they had money and prayed when they had none. They worked in the steamy heat of mills and when they knocked off shift and stepped outside, the cold gnawed through their clothes and cracked their bones like crazed china. You would have thought they would have bred, but they didn't. Some had no children at all, others had just one. These only children were precious, wouldn't you think? But one failed to marry, and another spent much of his life in an asylum.

So far, so good: what sort of family do you expect me to come from? All-singing, all-dancing? You'd just know they'd be tubercular, probably syphilitic, certifiably insane, dyslexic, paralytic, circumcised, circumscribed, victims of bad pickers in identity parades, mangled in industrial machinery, decapitated by forklift trucks, dental cripples, sodomites, sent blind by measles, riddled with asbestosis and domiciled downwind of Chernobyl. I assume you've read my new novel, *The Clean Slate*. I was working on the first draft at the time I decided to tackle Veronica. I had the theory that our family was bent on erasing itself, through divorce, elective celibacy and a series of gynecological catastrophes. "But I had children," Veronica said, bewildered. "I had you, didn't I?" Yes, Miss Bedjacket, you bet you did.

PROBABLY THE ONE thing you couldn't guess would be that I come from the drowned village. As a child I could hardly realize it myself. There is such a thing as portent-overload. Of course, I had the whole thing wrong. I misunderstood, and was prone to believe any rubbish people put my way.

Suppose that in Pompeii they had been given

an alert: time, but not much of it. They would have left—what—their oil jars, their weaving shuttles, their vessels of wine, dashed and dripping? I can't really picture it. I have never been to Italy. Suppose they had taken the warning and cleared out. That was how I thought Derwent would be: a Pompeii, a *Mary Celeste*.

I thought that the waters would rise, at first inch by inch, and creep under each closed door. And then swill about, aimless for a while, contained by linoleum. The first thing to go would be the little striped mats that people dotted about in those days. They were cheap things that would go sodden quickly. Beneath the lino would be stone flags. They would hold the water, like some denying stepmother, in a chilly embrace: it would be the work of a generation, to wear them down . . .

And so, thwarted, the water rises, like daughters or peasants denied, and plunges hungry fingers into the cupboards where the sugar and the flour are kept. The colander, resting on the stone sink, goes floating, the water recirculating through its holes. The half-shelled peapods bob, and eggcups, pans and chamber pots join the flotilla, as the water rises to the windowsills. A street's worth of tea brews itself.

Cakes of soap twirl twelve feet in the air, as if God were taking His Saturday soak. Gabbling like gossips on a picnic, the water surges, each hour higher by a foot, riser by riser creeping up the stairs and washing about the private items of Derbyshire persons, about their crisply ironed bloomers floating free of lavender presses: the lapping of wavelets hemming their plain knee-bands with lace. The flannel bedsheets are soaked, and the woolen blankets press on the mattresses like the weight of sodden sin: till the mad gaiety of the waters takes them over, and buoys them up in the finest easy style. The beds go sailing, tub chairs are coracles; the yellowed long johns with their attached vests wave arms and legs, cut free from conjugal arrangements, and swim like Captain Webb for liberty and France.

This was what I imagined. I thought some upriver valve was eased, and the flood began.

But in fact, the Ladybower dam was downvalley from Derwent village. There was no flood. Derwent died by drips. The rain fell and was bottled. The streams flowed and were contained. Ladybower closed her downstream valves and gradually the valley filled, in the course of nature, from the hillside streams and the precipitation of Pennine cloudbursts.

It filled slowly: as tears, if you cried enough, would fill a bowl.

VERONICA IS OLD now. She does and does not understand this. She could always entertain what they call "discontinuities." That is to say, slippages in time or sense, breaches between cause and effect. She can also entertain big fat sweating lies, usually told either to mystify people or to make her look good. I cannot tell you how many times she has misled me. I take the map of the Derwent valley to the light. I look back at her in the bed. I am sorry to say it—I wish I could say something else—but the plan of the reservoirs looks very like a diagrammatic representation of the female reproductive tract. Not a detailed one: just the kind you might give to medical students in their first year, or children who persist in inquiring. One ovary is the Derwent reservoir, the other is Hogg Farm. This second branch descends by Underbank to Cocksbridge. The other branch descends by Derwent Hall, past the school and the church, through the drowned village of Ashopton to the neck of the womb itself, at Ladybower House and Ladybower Wood: from there, to the Yorkshire Bridge weir, and the great world beyond.

What I know now is this: they demolished the village before they flooded it. Stone by stone it was smashed. They waited till the vicar had died before they knocked down the vicarage. I think of Derwent Hall and the shallow river that ran beside it, the packhorse bridge and the bridle path. They knocked down the hall and sold what they could. The drawing-room floor—oak boards—went for £40. The oak paneling was sold at 2s and 6d per square foot.

The village of Derwent had a church, St. James & St. John. There was a silver patten and an ancient font which the heathens at the hall had once used as a flowerpot. There was a sundial, and four bells, and 284 bodies buried in the churchyard. Nowhere could be found to take in these homeless bones, and the Water Board decided to bury them on land of its own. But the owner of the single house in the neighborhood raised such objections that the project was called off. It seemed they would have to go under the water, the dead men of Derwent.

But the churchyard at Bamford offered to house them, at the last push. They were exhumed one by one and their condition recorded—"complete skeleton," together with the nature of the subsoil, the state of the coffin and the depth at which they were found. The Water Board paid £500 and it was all settled up. A bishop said prayers.

Through 1944, the water rose steadily. By June

1945, only a pair of stone gateposts and the spire of the church could be seen.

When I was a child, people would tell me AS A FACT that in hot summers, the church spire would rise above the waters, eerie and desolate under the burning sun.

This is also untrue.

The church tower was blown up, in 1947. I have a photograph of it, blasted, crumbling, in the very act of joining the ruins below. But even if I showed this to Veronica, she wouldn't believe me. She'd only say I was persecuting her. She doesn't care for evidence, she seems to say. She has her own versions of the past, and her own way of protecting them.

Sometimes, to pass her time, Veronica knits something. I say "something" because I'm not sure if it has a future as a garment, or if she'll be wearing it anywhere out of here. She has a way of working her elbows that points her needles straight at me. When the nurse comes in she drops her weapons in the fold of the sheets and smiles, nicey-nice.

EVERY SATURDAY NIGHT, in the village where Veronica grew up, the English fought the Irish, at a specified street, called Waterside. As a child I used to play on this desolate spot. Bullrushes, reeds, swamps. (Be home for half past seven, Veronica always said.) I expect they were not serious fights. More like minuets with broken bottles. After all, next Saturday night they would have to do it all over again.

No; it was the Derbyshire people who were the wild bunch, in my opinion. Two brothers used to go around the pubs and advertise each other: my brother here will fight, run, leap, play cricket or sing, against any man in this county. The cricketer destroyed his career by felling the umpire with a blow in his only first-class match. Another brother, making his way home by moonlight, manslaughtered a person, tossed him over a wall and took ship for America. Another walked the bridle path from Glossop to Derwent in the company of a man who described himself as a doctor, but was later discovered to be an escaped and homicidal lunatic.

I like to imagine cross-connections. Perhaps this "doctor" was my psychotic Irish relative who was committed to a madhouse. I tried to run my theory past Veronica, and see if the dates fitted at all. She said she knew nothing about the bridle path, nothing about a lunatic. I was about to take her up on it when a nurse put her head around the door and said, "The doctor's here." I had to stand in the corridor. "Coffee?" some moron said, gesturing to two inches of sludge on a warm-plate. I just ignored the question. I put my head on the clear, clean plaster of the wall, which was painted in a neutral shade, like thought.

After a time, a doctor came out and stood by my elbow. He did a big act of *ahem* to attract my attention and when I continued to rest my head on the restful plaster he percussed my shoulder till I looked around. He was a short, irate, gray-haired man. He was smaller than me, in fact, and trying to impart news of some sort, almost certainly bad. As I write, the average height of an Englishwoman is a hair's breadth below five foot five. I barely scrape five three, and yet I tower over Veronica. A tear stings my eye. *So small.* Within the space of a breath, I witness myself: tear is processed, ticked, and shed.

The Ladybower Reservoir has a surface area of 504 acres. Its perimeter is thirteen miles approximately. Its maximum depth is 135 feet. One hundred thousand tons of concrete were used in its building, and one million tons of earth. I am suspicious of these round figures, as I am sure you are. But can I offer them to you, as a basis for discussion? When people talk of "burying the past," and "all water under the bridge," these are the kind of figures they are trading in.

Giving Up the Ghost

after her strange childhood, she came to be childless herself, and how the children who never saw the light have trailed her through the years and become part of her life and her fiction.

YOU COME TO this place, midlife. You don't know how you got here, but suddenly you're staring fifty in the face. When you turn and look back down the years, you glimpse the ghosts of other lives you might have led. All your houses are haunted by the person you might have been. The wraiths and phantoms creep under your carpets and between the warp and weft of your curtains, they lurk in wardrobes and lie flat under drawer liners. You think of the children you might have had but didn't. When the midwife says, "It's a boy," where does the girl go? When you think you're pregnant, and you're not, what happens to that child who has already formed in your mind? You keep it filed in a drawer of your consciousness, like a short story that wouldn't work after the opening lines.

In February of 2002, my godmother, Maggie, fell ill, and hospital visits took me back to my native village. After a short illness she died, at the age of almost ninety-five, and I returned again for her funeral. I had been back many times over the years, but on this occasion there was a particular route I had to take: down the winding road between the hedgerows and the stone wall, and up a wide unmade track which, when I was small, people called "the carriage drive." It leads uphill to the old school, now disused, then to the convent, where there are no nuns these days, then to the church. When I was a child this was my daily walk, once in the morning to school and once again to school after dinner—that meal which the south of England calls lunch. Retracing it as an adult, in my funeral black, I felt a sense of oppression, powerful and familiar. Just before the public road joins the carriage drive came a point where I was overwhelmed by fear and dismay. My eyes moved sideways, in dread, toward dank vegetation, tangled bracken: I wanted to say, stop here, let's go no further. I remembered how when I was a child, I used to think I might bolt, make a run for it, scurry back to the (comparative) safety of home. The point where fear overcame me was the point of no turning back.

Each month, from the age of seven to my leaving at eleven, we walked in line up the hill from the school to the church to go to confession and be forgiven for our sins. I would come out of church feeling, as you would expect, clean and light. This period of grace never lasted beyond the five minutes it took to get inside the school building. From about the age of four I had begun to believe I had done something wrong. Confession didn't touch some essential sin. There was something inside me that was beyond remedy and beyond redemption. The school's work was constant stricture, the systematic crushing of any spontaneity. It enforced rules that had never been articulated, and which changed as soon as you thought you had grasped them. I was conscious, from the first day in the first class, of the need to resist what I found there. When I met my fellow children and heard their yodeling cry—"Good mo-or-orning, Missis Simpson"—I thought I had come among lunatics; and the teachers, malign and stupid, seemed to me like the lunatics' keepers. I knew you must not give in to them. You must not answer questions which evidently had no answer, or which were asked by the keepers simply to amuse themselves and pass the time. You must not accept that things were beyond your understanding because they told you they were; you must go on trying to understand them. A state of inner struggle began. It took a huge expenditure of energy to keep your own thoughts intact. But if you did not make this effort you would be wiped out.

The story of my own childhood is a complicated sentence that I am always trying to finish, to finish and put behind me. It resists finishing, and partly this is because words are not enough; my early world was synesthetic, and I am haunted by the ghosts of my own sense impressions, which reemerge when I try to write, and shiver between the lines.

We are taught to be chary of early memories. Sometimes psychologists fake photographs in which a picture of their subject, in his or her childhood, appears in an unfamiliar setting, in places or with people whom in real life they have never seen. The subjects are amazed at first but then—in proportion to their anxiety to please—they oblige by producing a "memory" to cover the experience that they have never actually had. I don't know what this shows, except that some psychologists have persuasive personalities, that some subjects are imaginative, and that we are all told to trust the evidence of our senses, and we do it: we trust the objective fact of the photograph, not our subjective bewilderment. It's a trick, it isn't science; it's about our present, not about our past. Though my early memories are patchy, I think they are not, or not entirely, a confabulation, and I believe this because of their overwhelming sensory power; they come complete, not like the groping, generalized formulations of the subjects fooled by the photograph. As I say "I tasted," I taste, and as I say "I heard," I hear: I am not talking about a Proustian moment, but a Proustian cine-film. Anyone can run these ancient newsreels, with a bit of preparation, a bit of practice; maybe it comes easier to writers than to many people, but I wouldn't be sure about that. I wouldn't agree either that it doesn't matter what you remember, but only what you think you remember. I have an investment in accuracy; I would never say, "It doesn't matter, it's history now." I know, on the other hand, that a small child has a strange sense of time, where a year seems a decade, and everyone over the age of ten seems grown-up and of an equal age; so although I feel sure of what happened, I am less sure of the sequence and the dateline. I know, too, that once a family has acquired a habit of secrecy, memories begin to distort, because its members confabulate to cover the gaps in the facts; you have to make some sort of sense of what's going on around you, so you cobble together a narrative as best you can. You add to it, and reason about it, and the distortions breed distortions.

Still, I think people can remember: a face, a perfume—one true thing or two. Doctors used to say babies didn't feel pain; we know they were wrong. We are born with our sensibilities; perhaps we are conceived that way. Part of our difficulty in trusting ourselves is that in talking of memory we are inclined to use geological metaphors. We talk about buried parts of our past and assume the most distant in time are the hardest to reach: that one has to prospect for them with the help of a hypnotist, or psychotherapist. I don't think memory is like that: rather that it is like St. Augustine's "spreading limitless room." Or a great plain, a steppe, where all the memories are laid side by side, at the same depth, like seeds under the soil.

There is a color of paint that doesn't seem to exist anymore, that was a characteristic pigment of my childhood. It is a faded, rain-drenched crimson, like stale and drying blood. You saw it on paneled front doors, and on the frames of sash windows, on mill gates and on those high doorways that led to the ginnels between shops and gave access to their yards. You can still see it, on the more soot-stained and dilapidated old buildings, where the sandblaster hasn't yet been in to turn the black stone to honey: you can detect a trace of it, a scrape. The restorers of great houses use paint scrapes to identify the original color scheme of old salons, drawing rooms and staircase halls. I use this paint scrape—oxblood, let's call it—to refurbish the rooms of my childhood: which were otherwise dark green, and cream, and more lately a cloudy yellow, which hung about at shoulder height, like the aftermath of a fire.

When I am six years old I am put to bed in my parents' room in our new house at Brosscroft. So far only one bedroom of the house is habitable. My brother's cot stands against the window wall, the double bed occupies the center of the room, my small cream-painted bed is nearest the door. I lie under a tartan rug and my fingers twist and plait its fringe; plait, untwist, plait again: the wool is rough against my fingertips. I will myself into dreaming; I think about Red Indians and about Jesus, because Jesus is a thing I am exhorted to think about and I try, I do try. I think about my teepee, my tomahawk, my stocky bay horse who is standing even now, a striped blanket thrown over his back, ready to gallop me over the plains, into the red and dusty west. Then I think about how, downstairs perhaps even at this moment, my mother is putting on her coat and picking up her bag.

I believe she will leave in the night, abandon me. We should never have come to this house; we should have stayed as we were, with Grandma and Grandad down the road in their house at Bankbottom. Everything has gone wrong, so wrong that I don't know how to express it or understand it; I know that anyone who can flee disaster should do so, leaving the weak, the old and the babies behind in the wreckage. My mother is smart and fit and I think she will run, and take her chance on another life, a better life elsewhere: some princess-place, where her real family lives. With her ready smiles and her glowing red hair, she doesn't belong here, in these enclosing shadows: in these rooms that have filled silently with unseen, hostile observers.

My father, Henry, puts the baby to bed; this hour, when he is upstairs, seems like the time she would run. I think that, although it will almost kill me, I can bear it if I know the moment she goes, if I hear the front door close after her. But I can't bear it if I go downstairs in the morning to a cold and empty kitchen—warmed only by the glow of her Elvis poster, Elvis with his fat face beaming like the rising sun.

So I lie awake, listening, long after my father has crept downstairs, listening by the glow of the night-light to the sounds of the house. In the morning I am too tired to get up, but I must go to school because it is the law.

My arms and legs ache with a singing pain. The

doctor says it is growing pains. One day I find I cannot breathe. The doctor says if I didn't think about breathing I'd be able to do it. Frankly, he's sick of being asked what's wrong with me. He calls me Little Miss Neverwell. I am angry. I don't like being given a name. It's too much like power over me.

Persons shouldn't name you. Rumpelstiltskin.

Jack comes to visit us. He comes for his tea. These teas seem to be separate extra meals, in the big kitchen when the lights are on and the wild gardens fade into a dark bloom. We cook strange, frivolous dishes: dip eggs suddenly into bubbling fat, so that they fizz up like sea creatures, puff into pearls with translucent whitish legs. Is Jack coming today? I ask. Oh good. I am looking for someone to marry. It's a business I want to get settled up. I hope Jack might do, though it is a pity he is not my relative. He is just someone we know.

Down the hill at Bankbottom, they are talking about the latest novelty from Rome: the Pope says you can marry your second cousin! That means, people say, that Ilary could marry . . . if she wanted, of course . . . then they turn up various names of people I haven't heard of. I wish I had heard of them: I am keen for intelligence of these candidates; I am, I already know, the kind of person who would marry back into my own family, to keep us all together, to guarantee me a supply of familiar people, great-uncles needing Cheshire cheese, great-aunts with hats discussing in low voices while wielding their spoons over bowls of tinned peaches. I have a great-uncle who was in a military prison, "our Joe he is red-hot Labor," my grandmother says; I have a great-aunt who for money sold her long golden hair. Why are they great-uncles and great-aunts? Where is the next generation? Where are their children? Never born, or dead as babies. Poverty, my mother says, pneumonia. I write down "pneumonia." I don't know it is an illness, I think it is a cold wind that blows.

One day Jack comes for his tea and doesn't go home again. "Is he never going home?" I say. Night falls, on this new dispensation; it falls and falls on me. In subsequent weeks I become enraged, and am thrown into the Glass Place. Jack and my mother sit in the kitchen. I jump at the kitchen window and make faces at them. They draw the curtains and laugh. I try to crash the back door, but they have bolted it. I stamp and rage, outside in the cold. Rumpelstiltskin is my name.

YOU SHOULD NOT judge your parents. Mostly—this is the condition of parents—they were doing the best they could. They were addled and penniless and couldn't afford lawyers, they were every man's hand against them, they were—when you do the arithmetic—pathetically young. They couldn't see the wood for the trees or the way through the week from Monday to Friday. They were in love or they were enraged, they were betrayed or bitterly, bitterly disappointed, and just like our own generation they clutched at any chance to make it right, to make a change, to get a second chance: they beat off the fetters of logic and they gathered themselves up in weakness and despair and they spat in the eye of fate. This is what parents do. They believe love conquers all, or why would they have children, why would they have you? You should not judge your parents.

When you are six, seven, you do not know this. I feel that I myself have been judged: that I have committed an unnamed offense: that I have been sentenced, and that some unspecified penalty will be exacted, at short notice.

On a Saturday morning at Brosscroft I come down early and to my surprise Grandad is there. He is in the stone-shelved pantry, where the air is cold even in August. His tools are laid out there, because he's been helping fix up the house, but now he is wiping them and slotting them away in their canvas cradles. "What are you doing, Grandad?" I say. He says, "Sweetheart, I am packing these up, and going home."

I walk away, my heart sinking.

In the kitchen my mother grabs me. "What did he say to you?"

"Nothing."

"What?" She is burning, her cheeks flushed, her hair a conflagration. "Nothing? You mean he didn't speak to you?"

I see some furious new row in the making. I answer, without spirit, taking refuge in the literal: like the stupid messenger, bringing the bad news twice. "He said what he was doing. He said, sweetheart, I am packing these up, and going home."

Grandad walks away, down to Bankbottom, his spine unyielding, his neck stiff. Somewhere in the house a door slams. Glass trembles in its frames. Cupboards creak, the new mirror in the front room rattles its chain against its nail. The stairhead is lightless, the dead center of the house. I think I see someone turning the corner, down the corridor to the bedroom where my father, Henry, now sleeps in a single bed. The walls are yellow in that room and the curtains half drawn.

What happens now? We are talked about in the street. Some rules have been broken. A darkness closes about our house. The air becomes jaundiced and clotted, and hangs in gaseous clouds over the rooms. I see them so thickly that I think I am going to bump my head on them.

I have another brother now; where *do* they come from? They sleep in the main bedroom, the largest in my cream bed and the smallest in his cot. I am moved into my father's room, which is the yellow room down the passage. There is no natural light in the passage, only an overhead bulb that, by casting shadows, seems to thicken the murk rather than disperse it. I never walk but run between the stairhead and my bed. Our two puppies cry in the night. They are frightened. The man who comes to paint the stairhead is frightened, but I am not supposed to overhear about that.

The door key is missing. The house is turned over for it. Every surface is checked and every drawer. The floor is crawled with padding hands and sensitive knees. All visitors—but there are not many—have their brains trounced about it and their movements thoroughly interrogated. Some two days pass, and the key returns, placed on top of the china cabinet, dead center.

My mother stops going out to the shops. Only my godmother comes and goes between our house and Bankbottom. The children at school question me about our living arrangements, who sleeps in what bed. I don't understand why they want to know but I don't tell them anything. I hate going to school. Often I am ill with my growing pains and the breathing I am not supposed to think about and raging headaches that leave me hollow-eyed. When I go back to school after a few days nobody seems to know me and behind my own back I have gone up a class. The new teacher is called Miss Porter. I don't understand how she writes down the arithmetic. I've missed something. I put up my hand and say I don't understand. She stares at me in incredulity. Don't understand? Don't understand? What broil or civil mutiny is this? Why don't I just copy from the child next to me, like all the other little sillies? "You don't understand?" she repeats, her eyes popping with indignation. There is an outbreak of screeching giggles and adenoidal snorting.

Miss Porter is gone very soon. My ignorance remains.

Once a year, at school and church, we had Mission Sunday, when we sang about Africans and Indians. We called them Black Babies, and collected money for them. If you did well enough with fund-raising, you were allowed to own one. In the week before Mission Sunday we sang special hymns, their tunes undistinguished but their words thrilling. "For the infant wives and widows—Babies hurried to their graves . . ." How old did you need to be, to qualify as an infant wife? How did widowhood follow? And were the "babies hurried to their graves" the wives themselves, or their children?

The fact is, I might have got the words wrong; I may be producing some travesty of what was on the hymn sheet. At eight, I give up hearing. Whenever anyone speaks to me I say, "What?" While, irritated, they are repeating themselves, I gather myself, and recall to order the scattered pieces of my attention. Words are a blur to me; a moth's wing, flitting about the lamp of meaning. My own thoughts go at a different speed from that of human conversation, about two and a half times as fast, so I am always scrambling backward through people's speech, to work out which bit of which question I am supposed to be answering. I continue my habit of covert looking, out of the corner of my eye, and take up the art of sensing through the tips of my fingers. In the front room of the house at Brosscroft, Henry and I sit by lamplight, our chess game laid out before us. The babies upstairs are snorting in their sleep, my mother and Jack have gone—where? Gone dancing? I don't know. My long pale father sits folded into his chair, pushing wearily at a pawn; till on one inspired night, I the canning factory, where the slurries of unimaginable meats were processed into tins. My guardian angel followed, half a step behind, always and invisibly at my left shoulder. And God walked with me, I thought He did. You would imagine that I asked Him to show Himself and put an end to the events at Brosscroft: the slammings of doors in the night, the great gusts of wind that roared through the rooms. But my idea of God was different. He was not a magician and should not be treated in that way; should not be asked to alter things and fix things, like some plumber or carpenter, like my grandad with his tools rolled in their canvas cradles. I had come to my own understanding of grace, the seeping channel between persons and God: the slow, green and silted canal, between a person and the God inside them. Every sense is graceful, an agent of grace: touch, smell, taste. The grace of music is not for a child who says, "What?" My mother never plays the piano now, my father seldom; Jack is never seen to sit down to it, no doubt because he's Church of England. And I can't carry a tune; I'm told brutally about this. I can't sing fah soh lah tee doh without singing flat. You can pray for grace, but it is a thing that creeps in unexpectedly, like a draft. It is a thing you can't plan for. By not asking for it, you get it. For one year, I carried this knowledge, and carried a simple space for God inside me: a jagged space surrounded by light, a waiting space cut out of my solar plexus. I subsisted in this watchful waiting, a readiness. But what came wasn't God at all.

SOMETIMES YOU COME to a thing you can't write. You've written everything you can think of, to stop the story getting here. You know that, technically, your prose isn't up to it. You say then, very well: at least I know my limitations. So choose simple words; go slowly. But then you are aware that readers—any kind readers who've stayed with you—are bracing themselves for some revelation of sexual abuse. That's the usual horror. Mine is more diffuse. It wrapped a strangling hand around my life, and I don't know how, or what it was.

About the Author

Hilary Mantel was a renowned English writer who twice won the Booker Prize, for her bestselling novel *Wolf Hall* and its sequel, *Bring Up the Bodies*. The final novel of the Wolf Hall trilogy, *The Mirror & the Light*, debuted at #1 on the *New York Times* bestseller list and won worldwide critical acclaim. Mantel wrote seventeen celebrated books, including the memoir *Giving Up the Ghost*, and she was awarded the National Book Critics Circle Award for fiction, the Walter Scott Prize, the Costa Book Award, the Hawthornden Prize, and many other accolades. In 2014, Mantel was appointed Dame Commander of the Order of the British Empire (DBE). She died at age seventy in 2022.